Raggedy Ann and Andy
The First Treasury

Raggedy Ann and Andy
The First Treasury

Written
and
Illustrated
by
Johnny Gruelle

LEMON TREE PRESS

LEMON TREE PRESS · NEW YORK

Originally published in three volumes as:

RAGGEDY ANN AND ANDY AND THE CAMEL WITH THE WRINKLED KNEES Copyright © 1924 by John B. Gruelle; Copyright renewed 1951 by Myrtle Gruelle; Copyright 1951 by The Johnny Gruelle Company. Copyright, Great Britain, 1924 and 1951.

RAGGEDY ANN'S WISHING PEBBLE. Copyright © 1925 by the P.F. Volland Company, Joliet, U.S.A. Copyright, Great Britain, 1925.

RAGGEDY ANN AND THE PAPER DRAGON. Copyright © 1926 by P.F. Volland Company; Copyright renewed 1953 by Myrtle Gruelle.

A Lemon Tree Press Book
Published in the United States of America in 1982 by
Galahad Books
95 Madison Avenue
New York, N.Y. 10016

Published by arrangement with the Bobbs-Merrill Company, Inc.

Library of Congress Catalog Card Number 82-82741

ISBN 0-88365-661-2

PRINTED IN THE UNITED STATES OF AMERICA

CONTENTS

RAGGEDY ANN AND ANDY

and the Camel *with the* Wrinkled Knees

WRITTEN
AND
ILLUSTRATED
by
JOHNNY GRUELLE

Dedicated to
MARCELLA MATTHEWS

© JOHNNY GRUELLE

RAGGEDY ANN AND ANDY AND THE CAMEL WITH THE WRINKLED KNEES

RAGGEDY ANN and Raggedy Andy lay in their little doll beds, smiling up through the dark at the top of the play-house. It was very still and quiet in the play-house, but the Raggedys were not even a teeny-weeny speck lonesome, for they were thinking so many nice kindly thoughts. And, you know, when one thinks only lovely, kindly thoughts there is no time to become lonesome.

The play-house was an old piano-box and was all fixed up nice and cozy. There was an old rug upon the floor, two doll-beds, three little chairs, a table with pretty little play teacups and saucers and plates on it.

Raggedy Ann and Raggedy Andy lay upon the doll beds just where Marcella had left them that afternoon. One of Raggedy Ann's legs was twisted up over the other, but it wasn't the least bit uncomfortable, for Raggedy Ann's legs were stuffed with nice white, soft cotton and they could be twisted in every position and it did not trouble Raggedy Ann. No indeed! Neither Raggedy Ann nor Raggedy Andy had moved since they had been placed in the little doll beds, and now it was late at night. Marcella had forgotten to take the Raggedys in the house, but the Raggedys did not mind that either. They just smiled up at the top of the play-house and listened to the tiny sounds which came from the little creatures out in the grass and flowers.

At first Raggedy Ann was so busy thinking nice kindly thoughts she did not notice. Then when Johnny Cricket stopped squeeking upon his tiny fiddle Raggedy Ann knew something was about to happen. Her little candy heart with the words "I love you" printed upon it went pitty-pat against her nice cotton-stuffed body. And Raggedy Ann heard great big footsteps coming up the path, "Thump! thump! thump."

"Hmm!" Raggedy Ann whispered to Raggedy Andy, "I wonder who that can be?"

The great big footsteps came up to the play-house and went on, "Thump! thump! thump!"

Raggedy Andy jumped out of the little doll-bed and tiptoed to the door. The night was dark, but Raggedy Andy had two very good shoe-button eyes and as they were black shoe-button eyes, Raggedy Andy could see very well in the dark. And what do you think? Raggedy Andy saw a great big man reach right in one of the windows to the house and take something and run! The man ran right by the piano-box play-house and Raggedy Andy could have jumped out and touched him if he had wished. But Raggedy Andy was so surprised to see anyone reach in another person's house and take something, he could think of nothing to do or say; and so the man jumped over the back fence and ran across the field!

"Did you see, Raggedy Ann?" Raggedy Andy asked.

"Yes!" said Raggedy Ann, very decidedly, "we must run up to the house and find out what that man was doing!"

So, smoothing the wrinkles out of her apron and jiggling her legs to get the twists out of them, Raggedy Ann and Raggedy Andy ran up to the house and climbed upon a chair so that they could peep over the sill into the window.

When Raggedy Ann and Raggedy Andy peeped up over the window-sill, all the dolls remained very quiet, for they thought it was the man returning; but when they saw that it was Raggedy Ann's and Raggedy Andy's faces peeping in at them, they all jumped up and ran to them.

"What do you think, Raggedy Ann?" Uncle Clem cried. "Someone reached into the window and took the French doll! Wasn't that a rude thing to do?"

"My! My! My!" was all Raggedy Ann could say for awhile. Then after she sat and pulled her rag forehead down into a lot of wrinkles, Raggedy Ann was able to think of something to do.

"Raggedy Andy!" said Raggedy Ann. "We must run after the man and make him bring the French doll back here!"

"That is just what I was thinking!" Raggedy Andy replied, as he climbed upon the window-sill. "Come on, Raggedy Ann!"

Little Henny, the Dutch doll, wanted to go with Raggedy Ann and Raggedy Andy, but Raggedy Ann said, "No Henny, you must stay here and take care of the rest of the dolls! You see, you are the only man left!" This pleased Henny so much he tried to stick out his chest so far that he fell over backwards and cried, "M-a-m-m-a!" in his quavery voice.

Raggedy Andy knew just which way the strange man had run, for he had watched him, so after jumping from the window and catching hold of her hand, Raggedy Andy and Raggedy Ann raced through the yard, climbed through a hole in the fence and scooted across the field.

Raggedy Ann and Raggedy Andy ran until they came to the center of the field, and all the way they had followed the man's trail where he had bent down the grass and field flowers. But when tney came to tne center of the field, the grass and flowers were not bent down, and Raggedy Ann and Raggedy Andy stopped.

"Now isn't that strange, Raggedy Ann?" Raggedy Andy asked. "He hasn't gone beyond here and still he isn't here!"

"Then if he isn't here," Raggedy Ann answered, "he must have gone on, Raggedy Andy."

"But how could he, Raggedy Ann, when we can see that his footsteps end right here?" Raggedy Andy asked.

"Why! He must have gone up in the air, that's what,

Raggedy Andy!" Raggedy Ann replied.

"Then we can follow him no farther!" Raggedy Andy cried, as he dropped his rag arms to his side and looked very sad. "What shall we do, Raggedy Ann?"

"Let's sit down and think as hard as we can, Raggedy Andy," said Raggedy Ann. "Even if we rip sixteen stitches out of our heads thinking so hard, let's try to think of what we had better do."

So Raggedy Andy sat down beside her and threw one arm about Raggedy Ann's shoulder. And there they sat and thought and thought, just as hard as they could, until Raggedy Andy felt five stitches rip in his rag head and Raggedy

© JOHNNY GRUELLE

Ann felt five stitches rip in her rag head, but neither one could think of anything to do.

"For," Raggedy Ann said out loud, "if we can't fly, how can we follow him?" This also puzzled Raggedy Andy and he said so.

Then Raggedy Ann and Raggedy Andy held their breaths; for, coming towards them through the flowers and tall grasses they saw a dim, greenish blue light. And as the pretty light (it was just like a Will-o'the wisp) came up to them they saw that a pretty Fairy carried it at the end of a waving stick! No wonder Raggedy Ann and Raggedy Andy held their breaths, she was such a pretty little Fairy creature and it seemed so strange that at last they were getting to see a real for-sure live Fairy. Very often all the dolls had wished that they might see a Fairy. Now a very lovely Fairy stood before Raggedy Ann and Raggedy Andy! May be, very often, beautiful Fairies stand in front of us and whisper to us but we are unable to see or hear them; who knows? But Raggedy Ann and Raggedy Andy could not

only see this pretty little Fairy creature, but they could hear her too.

"Why do you hold your breaths, Raggedy Ann and Raggedy Andy?" the pretty little Fairy asked, and there was a sly little tinkle to her voice which made Raggedy Ann and Raggedy Andy know that the pretty little Fairy knew why they held their breaths.

But Raggedy Ann laughed and said, "We are holding our breaths, because we have never seen a real for-sure live beautiful Fairy before, and we did not wish to frighten you away." And this made the pretty little Fairy laugh right out loud.

"Of course, I knew why, Raggedy Ann and Raggedy Andy," she said. "But now that we are good friends, please do not hold your breaths any longer. For, I know why you are sitting out in the center of the field and I know just how you can follow the man who took the French doll."

"I thought maybe the man might be Santa Claus," Raggedy Ann said. "But then after I had ripped five stitches in my rag head thinking, I knew it could not be Santa who took the French doll, for he only takes dolls when they need fixing up and the French doll was always kept just as good as new. Except when Marcella fed her chocolate candy and got chocolate around the French doll's mouth."

"No, it wasn't Santa Claus," Raggedy Andy said.

"No, it wasn't Santa Claus," the pretty little Fairy agreed. "But now the thing to do is for you two to follow the strange man. And in order to do that, you must be able to fly, for he flew away from here, you know."

"That is just what I thought," Raggedy Ann said.

"Raggedy Ann can think ever so much better than I can," Raggedy Andy told the Fairy. "For Raggedy Ann has a lovely candy heart and I guess that's why."

The pretty little Fairy laughed at this and said, "Granny Balloon-spider lives near here and I will ask her to build you a nice fluffy balloon so that you can follow the man who took the French doll." And the pretty little Fairy led the way

until they came to a cunning little cottage and there stood Granny out on the porch waiting for them.

"Will you spin Raggedy Ann and Raggedy Andy a nice fluffy balloon in which they can fly after the man who took the French doll?" the pretty little Fairy asked Granny.

"Indeed, I will be very glad to spin them a balloon!" Granny replied. "But in order to carry them through the air I will have to spin such a large balloon that it will take me several days."

"Oh, I shall fix that all right, Granny," the pretty little Fairy laughed. "If you will bring your little spinning-wheel out here on the porch, I will say a magic charm over it, and you will be able to spin the balloon in a very short time!"

© JOHNNY GRUELLE

So, when Granny Balloon-spider brought the cunning little spinning-wheel out upon the porch, the pretty little Fairy waved her fairy light over it and sang, "Little cunning spinning-wheel, spin and whir and sing, spin a silken balloon to carry Raggedy Ann and Raggedy Andy up in the air in search of the French doll!" And Granny put her little red-slippered foot upon the treadle of the spinning-wheel and the cunning little spinning-wheel looked like solid silver it whirled so fast. And before you could recite, "The house that Jack built" the little silken balloon was finished.

The pretty little Fairy fastened a silken thread to Raggedy Ann's hand and to Raggedy Andy's hand and touched the silken balloon with her fairy light; then the silken balloon rose in the air and carried Raggedy Ann and Raggedy Andy with it.

"Good bye and thank you!" Raggedy Ann and Raggedy Andy called down to the little Fairy and Granny Balloon-spider, and the little Fairy waved her fairy light until the silken balloon had carried our two friends way up above a feathery cloud.

And as the gentle breeze blew them along, ever so gently, Raggedy Ann and Raggedy Andy twisted and swung about at the end of the silken threads tied to their rag hands.

"Isn't it lovely, Raggedy Andy?" Raggedy Ann asked. "I can scarcely believe we are not dreaming!"

"It is ever so much nicer than floating on water!" Raggedy Andy replied.

CHAPTER TWO

RAGGEDY ANN and Raggedy Andy floated through the air, carried along by the silken balloon until they could see the great, round, golden Sun peeping up over the rim of the Earth.

"Good morning, Mr. Sun!" Raggedy Ann laughed; but of course the Sun did not answer, for he was thousands of miles away and did not hear. Then Raggedy Ann noticed that they were drifting closer and closer to the ground, and after awhile, the silken balloon caught in a low branch of a tree and there Raggedy Ann and Raggedy Andy hung, dangling by the silken cords the Fairy had tied to their hands.

"Well, here we are!" laughed Raggedy Andy, "But how will we get down to the ground?"

"That is what has been bothering me, too," Raggedy Ann said. "Of course it would not hurt either of us to drop from here to the ground, if we could only untie the silken cords the Fairy tied about our hands."

And so Raggedy Ann and Raggedy Andy hung there dangling and twisting about until finally Raggedy Andy laughed and asked, "Do you know what, Raggedy Ann?"

"No, what, Raggedy Andy?" Raggedy Ann asked in reply.

"Why," Raggedy Andy said. "If we can't get down, then let's get up!" And with this, Raggedy Andy twisted his legs up over the limb and was soon sitting upon it. Then he pulled Raggedy Ann up beside him. When they had their hands in front of them, it was an easy matter to untie the silken cord.

"There we are!" laughed Raggedy Andy. "Now all we have to do, is to jump from the tree and continue our search for the French doll!" So Raggedy Ann and Raggedy Andy stood up on the limb and took hold of hands.

"One for the money, two for the show, three to make ready and here she goes!" they both sang and jumped. "Blump! Blump!" they struck against the ground and

©
JOHNNY GRUELLE

rolled over.

"Didn't hurt me a speck!" laughed Raggedy Ann.

"Me either!" laughed Raggedy Andy as he sat up and dusted his clothes.

"Ha!" came a voice from behind the tree, and as they looked Raggedy Ann and Raggedy Andy saw the queerest creature come walking towards them. It was a Camel, made out of canton flannel and stuffed with sawdust, but he had evidently been played with so much, his legs were no longer straight and stiff. Instead, the canton flannel Camel's legs were wrinkled and so out of press, it seemed that he would pitch forward upon his head at each step. When the Camel came up to Raggedy Ann and Raggedy Andy, he sat down beside them, and in doing this his knees gave way with him and he rolled over upon his side.

"Wup!" Raggedy Andy said, as he helped the Camel to sit up, "You almost fell over that time."

"Indeed I did," the Camel laughed, "My legs are not what they used to be. See how wrinkled my knees are?"

Raggedy Andy tried to smooth out the wrinkles in the Camel's knees, but the Camel smiled and said, "It doesn't do a bit of good trying to get the wrinkles out. They come right back in again just as soon as I stand up," he continued. "You see when I was brand-new, I was made with sticks in each leg, but these sticks were the sticks which are made to put in meat when it is tied up and roasted, and each stick had a point on the end. Well, sir, after I had been played with for a few weeks, those pointed sticks punched right up through my back and I wasn't safe for a little boy to play with. So the little boy's mother pulled the meat sticks out of my legs, and that let me sag down until my knees grew terribly wrinkled!"

"That is too bad!" Raggedy Ann said, as she patted the Camel's head.

"Four bad, my dear!" the Camel corrected.

"Oh, I didn't mean the number of legs you had, I meant that I felt sorry," Raggedy Ann laughed.

"Ha! Ha! Now I understand," the Camel laughed. "But really, it isn't quite as bad as one would imagine, for when I had sticks in my legs I had to walk stiff-legged and that wasn't a speck graceful, but now, I can walk along very softly without going 'thump! thump! thump!' And it is ever so much more comfortable when I lie down now than it was when I had to stick my legs out stiffly at the side."

"When you said, 'Thump! thump! thump!' it reminded me of something!" said Raggedy Ann.

"What was it?" the Camel with the wrinked knees asked.

Then Raggedy Ann told him how she had heard the man's footsteps go "thump! thump! thump!" the night before.

The Camel with the wrinkled knees scratched his head with the loppiest leg and asked, "Was he a large man, with two legs and two arms, dressed in clothing?"

"The very man!" cried Raggedy Andy, "I was looking out of the play-house door when the man reached in the window and took her!"

"Then, I am sure I can tell you how to find him!" the Camel with the wrinkled knees cried, excitedly. "For I know it is the same man who took me out of the little boy's play house one night. I ran away from him. Some day I'm going back home, for I had lots of good times with my little boy owner!"

"Hurry and tell us how to find the mean man, please!" Raggedy Ann begged. "For we must rescue the French doll and return home as soon as we can."

"Well," the Camel with the wrinkled knees said, "Do you see that great big tree way over there?"

"Yes!" Raggedy Ann and Raggedy Andy both cried.

"Well," the Camel said. "You mustn't go that way! You must go this way. Then when you get to this way you must turn and go that way until you come to this way again. Then take the first turn this way, until you come to that way and after walking that way ten minutes you turn and go this way. Then you are there."

"Hmm!" mused Raggedy Ann and Raggedy Andy, "We should be able to find it in the dark after such a *good* description of the way to reach there!"

"That's the funny part of the whole thing," the Camel with the wrinkled knees laughed. "I ran away from the man at night when it was very, very dark, and I could easily find my way back in the dark, but I would get lost in the daytime!"

"Then I guess we will have to go alone," Raggedy Ann said.

"I'd like to return with you and help rescue the French doll," the Camel with the wrinkled knees said. "But I know I should never be able to find it in the light."

"Maybe if you would shut your eyes you could lead us to the place where the man lives," Raggedy Andy suggested.

"Ha!" the Camel laughed, "How can I shut my eyes, when they are shoe buttons just like Raggedy Ann's?"

"I never thought of that!" Raggedy Andy said. "But be quiet—Raggedy Ann is trying to think of some way!"

"I never said a word!" the Camel replied

"Yes, you did!" Raggedy Andy said. "You are talking now, and it disturbs Raggedy Ann while she is thinking! So please remain very quiet and don't even cough, because sometimes Raggedy Ann rips a great many stitches out of her head and the cotton stuffing shows after she has thought

© JOHNNY GRUELLE

real, real hard. Just sit quietly and wait, as I am doing, and pretty soon you will be surprised to find out how well Raggedy Ann can think. Why, I remember one time when we were having a—"

"I shan't say a word!" the Camel promised.

"Yes, you say that you will not say anything, but just the minute you say that, can't you see that you are saying something?"

"Well! How can you tell that I shan't say a word unless I tell you that I shan't say a word? Just you tell me that, Mister Raggedy Andy!" the Camel replied.

"This is no time to guess riddles," Raggedy Andy said. "If we were guessing riddles, I know one I'll bet a nickel you could never, never guess. But what I have asked you to do is to remain very quiet, for the more quiet you remain the sooner Raggedy Ann will be able to think of something to do."

"Then I shall remain positively quiet, Raggedy Andy, so let's not quarrel about it."

"I shan't quarrel with you," Raggedy Andy replied, "But you continually start—"

"I've thought of a good scheme!" Raggedy Ann cried, as she jumped to her feet. "If the Camel with the wrinkled knees cannot shut his eyes and if he cannot show us the way to the man's place in the daytime, then we must cover his eyes with a hanky. Then it will be just the same as if it were dark!"

"I only see one thing wrong with your idea, Raggedy Ann," the Camel said.

"What is it?" Raggedy Ann asked.

"Why," the Camel replied, "If we tie something over the man's eyes, don't you see we will be where he is without having to go there!"

"Silly!" Raggedy Andy cried, "Raggedy Ann means to tie something over your eyes instead of the man's eyes!"

"Oh!" the Camel with the wrinkled knees laughed, as Raggedy Ann tied her pocket hanky over the Camel's shoe-button eyes, "Now I see!"

When Raggedy Ann had finished tying her pocket hanky over the Camel's eyes she said, "Now we had better start."

"Turn me around three times," the Camel said. "So that I won't get all mixed up in my directions. Then you had better get upon my back, for I shall go just as fast as I possibly can and you may not be able to keep up with me."

Raggedy Ann turned the Camel with the wrinkled knees around three times, then she and Raggedy Andy climbed upon his back.

"Hold tight!" the Camel cried, "Here we go!" and with this he started walking, slowly at first, then faster and faster, until soon his wabbly, wrinkled legs were hitting the ground, "Clumpity clumpity, clumpity," and he was running surprisingly fast.

Raggedy Ann and Raggedy Andy held on, even though the Camel bounced them up and down a great deal as he jumped along.

"Where are we now?" the Camel asked, after he had run steadily for five minutes. Raggedy Ann and Raggedy Andy looked about them.

"Why!" they cried in surprise, "We are right back where we started from! You must have run in a large circle!"

"Maybe I did," the Camel replied, "Of course I cannot see where I am running, but I know perfectly well that I am going in the right direction."

"But, Mr. Camel!" Raggedy Ann exclaimed, as she slid from the Camel's back, "How can you be going in the right direction when you return to the place where we started from? Can't you see, that we might just as well have stood still and saved you all that running?"

"Maybe we had better try it again!" the Camel advised, "I am certain that I am not mistaken!"

So Raggedy Ann and Raggedy Andy again climbed upon the Camel's back and again the Camel carried them at a run for five minutes.

"Now where are we?" the Camel asked.

"We are right where we started from!" Raggedy Andy cried, "I don't believe you know where you are trying to go!"

"Of course I don't!" the Camel agreed. "But do not let that fool you! I have run exactly the same as I did when I came from the man's place!"

"A-hhhhh!" Raggedy Ann exclaimed. "I know what's the trouble, Mr. Camel! You have been running just the same as you did when you came from the man's place so in order to return to the man's place, don't you see—you must run backwards!"

"Of course!" the Camel chuckled. "It's funny I didn't think of running backwards before!" The Camel couldn't run quite as fast backwards as he did frontward, but he covered a lot of ground. After running backwards for five minutes, the Camel again asked, "Where are we now?"

"I do not know!" Raggedy Ann and Raggedy Andy both answered.

"Then," said the Camel, "We must be getting somewhere!"

CHAPTER THREE

WHEN the Camel with the wrinkled knees had rested for a few minutes, he again started running backwards and was jumping along very fast when Raggedy Ann cried suddenly, "Whoa!"

The Camel immediately stopped and Raggedy Ann and Raggedy Andy, not expecting him to stop so suddenly, rolled off his back and turned over and over in the grass.

"Why did you cry, 'Whoa'?" the Camel wished to know when Raggedy Ann and Raggedy Andy had picked themselves up and came back to him.

"There's a little girl standing over there crying," Raggedy Ann said. "We must go over and see what is the trouble."

Raggedy Ann took the hanky from the Camel's eyes and the three walked over towards the little girl. When the little girl saw them she stopped crying and said, "Don't come any closer, or the Snap Dragons will catch you!"

"Hmm," mused Raggedy Andy. "Snap Dragons—who's afraid of Snap Dragons? Not me!" And with that, he walked right up to the little girl.

Raggedy Ann, when she saw that nothing happened to Raggedy Andy, also walked up to the little girl.

"The Snap Dragons are nothing but flowers," Raggedy Andy said, and indeed this was true, for all about the little girl's feet pretty flowers were twined.

"How long have you been standing here, little girl?" Raggedy Ann asked.

"For a long, long time," the little girl replied. "Every time I try to walk away the Snap Dragons catch my feet and hold me."

"Nonsense!" Raggedy Andy exclaimed. "Catch hold of my hand and we will walk over to where there are no Snap Dragons!"

But when the little girl did this and Raggedy Andy tried

© JOHNNY GRUELLE

to walk, he found that the Snap Dragons also fastened themselves around his legs.

And when Raggedy Ann caught hold of Raggedy Andy's hand and pulled, the Snap Dragons wrapped themselves around her feet and held her.

"You see!" the little girl cried, "Now you are prisoners too, and we will never get away from them!"

When the Camel saw that Raggedy Ann had become a prisoner too, he turned and walked still farther away from the Snap Dragons and sat down to think it over. Although the Camel with the wrinkled knees sat and tried to think for a long, long time, he could not think of a way to rescue his

friends from the Snap Dragons. Even though he scratched his head with his left hind leg he could not think of a way.

"I wonder how long we will have to stay here before we are rescued?" Raggedy Ann mused out loud.

"We may have to stay here years and years!" the little girl cried. Then she told Raggedy Ann and Raggedy Andy all about herself. "My name is Jenny," the little girl began, "and my brother's name is Jan. We used to live in a little cottage right in the center of the deep, deep woods. The little cottage was no larger than a big dry-goods box, but that was large enough for Jan and me. You see, we lived there all by ourselves."

"Didn't you have a mamma or a daddy?" Raggedy Ann asked in surprise.

"No," Jenny replied, as she brushed a tear from her eye. "Mamma and Daddy went over to see Gran'ma one day, and they never came back. So Jan and I went into the deep, deep woods to hunt for mamma and daddy, but we could not find them. And we could not find our way back home so when we discovered the dear little cottage, which was no larger than a dry-goods box, Jan and I lived there!"

"But where is Jan now?" Raggedy Andy wanted to know.

"I was just about to tell you!" Jenny replied. "In the deep, deep woods, as you surely must know, there are Gnomes and Elves and Fairies! And besides the Fairies and Gnomes and Elves there are other little creatures. Sometimes Jan and I could not see the little Fairies and Gnomes and Elves or other little creatures, but we could hear them singing, or laughing or talking. Then at other times, we could see them, but we could not hear them. Then sometimes we could see and hear them, too. And so, one day, Jan went out in back of the cunning little cottage to get a pail of water from the spring and when he came back into the house there was the queerest little man-creature with him we had ever seen!"

"What was it?" Raggedy Ann asked.

"It was a Loonie!" Jenny answered. "And if you have never seen a Loonie, do not ever long to see one, for they are not as cunning as Elves and Gnomes or Fairies! Instead, Loonies have large eyes which roll around every which way, and long red noses and crooked legs. They are funny-looking little creatures and really make you laugh when you see them. And that is just what Jan and I did, when the little Loonie walked into our little house with Jan. And do you know?" Jenny said, "When we laughed at the little Loonie, it made him so angry, he just bounced all around our little house and yelled at us."

"I'll just bet, when you laughed at him, that made him hopping mad," said Raggedy Andy.

"Yes," Jenny said, "That is just what happened, and we did not know that such a small creature could be so strong. And before either Jan or I could do a thing, the little Loonie caught Jan's feet and dragged him right out of the little cottage and away through the woods!"

"Couldn't Jan catch hold of bushes, so the Loonie couldn't pull him?" Raggedy Andy asked.

"Oh, yes," Jenny replied. "But the little Loonie was so strong, he just pulled Jan's hands away from the bushes and ran with him so fast, I could not follow." And Jenny began crying again.

"Please do not cry," Raggedy Ann begged, as she wiped the little girl's eyes with her apron, "We will help you find Jan. And when we catch the Loonie we will spank him good. Won't we, Raggedy Andy?"

"Indeed we will," Raggedy Andy promised.

"And after I had searched and searched for Jan, all through the deep, deep woods, and could not find him, I came out across this field, and just the minute I stopped amongst the Snap Dragons, they twined around my feet and I could not move."

"And you have never found out where the Loonie took Jan?" Raggedy Andy asked.

"I suppose he took Jan to the Town of the Loonies," Jenny answered. "But even though I asked everyone I met in the deep woods, they could not tell me how to get to Loonie Town."

"Perhaps someone could have told you," Raggedy Ann suggested. "But maybe they knew that if you went there alone, you would be captured and made a prisoner just as Jan was."

Jenny was just about to reply to Raggedy Ann when she saw a funny old Horse, not much larger than the Camel with the wrinkled knees.

"What are you all standing around for?" the old Horse asked as he came up to the edge of the patch of Snap Dragons. "Is there going to be a parade?"

© JOHNNY GRUELLE

"You'd better come over here and sit down with me," the Camel with the wrinkled knees called. "I am trying to think."

The old Horse walked over to where the Camel sat and lay down beside him. "My, I'm tired," the Horse sighed.

"Have you walked far?" the Camel with the wrinkled knees asked.

"No, not very far," the old Horse replied, "but you see, I am so old, the least bit of exercise wears me out and I have to lie down and rest."

"I am trying to think of a way to rescue my friends there," the Camel said, as he pointed to Raggedy Ann, Raggedy Andy and Jenny.

"Have they been captured?" the tired old Horse wanted to know.

"Certainly," the Camel replied, "They are standing right in a whole lot of Snap Dragons and can't get away."

"Hmm," the tired old Horse said, as he slowly got to his feet and stretched, "I will look into this." And from his pants pocket he took a case and from the case a pair of old-fashioned spectacles.

When he had put the spectacles on his nose he walked up and looked at the Snap Dragons. "Well, I'll declare!" he cried as he jumped back suddenly and upset the Camel. "Just put on my spectacles," he said, as he handed them to the Camel.

When the Camel with the wrinkled knees had the spectacles on his nose and looked at the Snap Dragons, he turned and ran as hard as his wobbly legs would let him. And the tired old Horse ran after him. After an exciting chase clear across the field, the tired old Horse finally managed to catch the Camel's string tail between his teeth and stop him.

"Silly!" the tired old Horse cried, as he took his spectacles away from the Camel, "I didn't mean to give you the spectacles to keep. I just loaned them to you." And the tired old Horse placed the spectacles on his own nose and slowly walked back towards Raggedy Ann and the others.

"I did not mean to keep your spectacles," the Camel with the wrinkled knees tried to explain, as he followed the tired old Horse.

"Then why did you run?" the tired old Horse asked, "That's what I want to know."

"Because," the camel replied. "Those are not Snap Dragon flowers at all! They are real live Dragons! Chinese Dragons!"

The tired old Horse turned and looked the Camel with the wrinkled knees up and down, from his feet to his head. Then shaking his head sadly the tired old Horse walked amongst the Snap Dragons and laid down.

"Now you are in a pickle too!" Raggedy Andy cried. "How can you rescue us when you are captured just the same as we are?"

The tired old Horse rolled over upon his back and kicked his four feet in the air, "If I can roll all the way over, I'm worth a hundred dollars," he said.

"I wouldn't give five cents for you now!" the Camel cried, as he sat down at the edge of the clump of Snap Dragons.

After kicking about for a few minutes, the tired old Horse succeeded in rolling over. "Whee!" the tired old Horse cried, "I'm worth a hundred dollars!" and with that he began prancing and kicking up his heels and frisking all about Raggedy Ann and Raggedy Andy and Jenny.

"You be careful there, Mister," Raggedy Ann cautioned, "First thing you know, you'll kick Jenny!"

CHAPTER FOUR

THE tired old Horse stopped kicking up his heels and walked up to Jenny and looked at her intently through his spectacles. Then he took them off and wiped them with a red bandanna handkerchief. "Ha!" he cried, when he looked at Jenny without his spectacles, "I thought I recognized you. You used to live in the little cottage in the center of the deep, deep woods, didn't you?"

"Why, yes," Jennie replied. "How did you know?"

"Because," the tired old Horse said, "I used to be driven through the deep, deep woods every day, to haul wood for my master until I got so old and tired I couldn't haul wood any more; then my master turned me loose to live by myself and he got a young horse to take my place. I used to see you almost every day. You and Jan," the Horse continued. "Why don't you return to the cunning little cottage?"

"Because," Raggedy Andy replied, "can't you see, Jenny has been captured by the Snap Dragons, and so have we, and so have you."

"Nonsense!" the tired old Horse laughed. "All you have to do is just walk away from the Snap Dragons like this."

"Huh!" the Camel with the wrinkled knees cried, when he saw that the tired old Horse couldn't budge. "Now you are in for it, just like the rest of them."

The tired old Horse looked at his feet and all about him in a surprised sort of way. Then a broad smile spread over his kindly face and he put on his spectacles. When the spectacles were firmly placed upon his nose, the Horse ran in circles around Raggedy Ann, Raggedy Andy and Jenny.

"There! You see?" the tired old Horse said, as he stopped in front of Jenny, "I couldn't budge before, because I did not have on my magic spectacles, and the Snap Dragons looked just like Snap Dragons! But now that I have on my Magic spectacles, the Snap Dragons are only Violets, so of course they can not get around my feet and hold me!"

"Then will we have to wear magic spectacles before we can get away from the Snap Dragons?" Jenny wished to know.

"Oh, no," the tired old Horse replied, "I shall eat all the Violets which look to you like Snap Dragons. In that way, I shall have a fine meal and they won't tangle around your feet." And without another word, the tired old Horse started eating, and in a short time Jenny was able to walk over and sit down beside the Camel with the wrinkled knees.

"My, goodness," she said, "It feels good to be able to sit

down again."

It did not take the tired old Horse very long to eat the Violets around Raggedy Ann's and Raggedy Andy's feet and so, very soon, they were all standing together beside the Camel with the wrinkled knees.

The tired old Horse took off his spectacles and put them in his pocket.

"Now," he said, as he rubbed his forefeet together, just as a man does when he is about to say something interesting. "We will talk about Jenny and Jan."

"We must help Jenny find Jan, don't you think so?" Raggedy Ann asked.

"Indeed, that is just what I was going to say!" cried the tired old Horse. "When I used to haul wood through the deep, deep woods past Jenny's little cottage I used to see her and Jan playing there together almost every day."

"But I do not remember seeing you," Jenny laughed.

"There was a good reason, my dear," the tired old Horse laughed. "At that time I was just an ordinary horse and you belong to some tribe of Fairies, or Gnomes, or Elves, or something. Anyway, I could see you, but you could not see me, nor could you see my master or the cart of wood I used to haul. Could you?"

"No. I do not remember seeing the cart, or your master," Jennie replied.

"There, you see!" the tired old Horse said to Raggedy Ann. "Well, one day I was hauling wood for my master and I saw the Loonie come out of your little cottage dragging Jan. And although I wanted to run after the Loonie and rescue Jan, I could not do so, because I was hitched to the cart. But I watched until I saw right where the Loonie took Jan, and I'll bet sixteen nickels I can show you right where he took Jan inside a great tree."

"Then let us waste no time in going there!" Raggedy Andy cried, as he jumped to his feet. "There is no telling, perhaps Jan has been in prison all this time."

"I will take Jenny upon my back, because she is the heaviest and the Camel can take Raggedy Ann and Raggedy Andy upon his back, and we will run like everything until we come to the deep, deep woods."

"But," said the Camel with the wrinkled knees, "I was taking Raggedy Ann and Raggedy Andy to show them where the man had taken the French Doll. And the only way I can find the place is to be blindfolded and run backwards, and if I do that, how can I follow you, Mister Horse?"

"I tell you what let's do," Raggedy Ann suggested. "Let us do as the tired old Horse says, then when we rescue Jan from the Loonies, we will all search for the man who carried away the French doll, Babette."

This was agreeable to the Camel with the wrinkled knees and soon he and the tired old Horse were racing across the fields towards the deep, deep woods. In a few moments they came to the deep, deep woods and raced down a winding path until they came to the little cottage where Jenny and Jan had lived. And a few yards beyond this, the tired old Horse sat down under a great tree.

"Whew!" he cried, as he took off his hat and fanned himself, "That surely made me tired! Well, anyway, here is the tree in which the Loonie took Jan."

"And if I am not mistaken," the Camel with the wrinkled knees said, "this is also the place where I was running backwards to. Just put your handkerchief over my eyes and let me see."

When Raggedy Ann had bound her handkerchief over the Camel's eyes, he said, "Yes, sir, this is the very spot!" And he handed Raggedy Ann her hanky.

"What I can't understand is how the Loonie could drag Jan into the tree when there isn't a single hole in the tree," Raggedy Andy said. Everyone walked around the large tree, but there appeared no hole of any sort in the tree.

"Are you sure you haven't made a mistake, Mister Horse?" Raggedy Andy asked.

"I am sure," the tired old Horse replied. "And besides, doesn't the Camel say this is the place he was trying to run to?"

The tired old Horse took off his hat again and scratched his head. "Ah," he said, "I have it. We must blindfold the Camel with the wrinkled knees and follow him into the tree; for I am sure it is a magic tree, or at least the entrance into the tree is covered with magic and we are unable to see it."

So Raggedy Ann again blindfolded the Camel with the

wrinkled knees and without waiting for the others, he backed into the tree and disappeared. And where the Camel with the wrinkled knees had backed into the tree, there was no hole of any sort to be seen.

"O, dear!" Raggedy Ann cried when the last of the Camel disappeared into the tree. "Now he has gone and we shall be unable to follow!"

For as she spoke she walked up to where the Camel had disappeared and felt of the tree; it was just as solid there as at any other place upon its surface.

"We should all have held onto the Camel's nose," the Horse said. "For I guess there is something magic about the Camel which lets him walk right through things when he is blindfolded."

"I guess there is nothing to do except wait outside here until the Camel finds we are not with him. Then perhaps he will return," Raggedy Andy said. Presently the Camel poked his head out of the tree trunk. "Where are you?" he asked.

"Right where you left us," Raggedy Ann replied. "Let us all catch hold of your nose and perhaps we can all get into the tree." And when everyone had crowded around the Camel and had caught hold of his nose, the Camel backed into the tree and the others went with him.

The tree seemed very much larger, when our friends were once inside, and appeared as a great room. Over at one side of the great room there was a slab of stone with a ring in it.

"It must be a trap-door," Raggedy Andy said as he caught hold of the ring and tried to raise the stone.

"Let us all catch hold of the ring," Raggedy Ann suggested. "Perhaps we can lift it." But though all pulled with all their might, the stone would not be lifted.

"This must be the way down into Loonie Land," the tired old Horse said. "Let us sit down and see what we can think of. There must be a way to open this trap-door."

And as he finished speaking, the tired old Horse sat down upon the stone. And as he sat down rather hard, the stone lowered with him and he went tumbling down below. The others could not see where the tired old Horse fell to, for the stone immediately closed after he had disappeared, but they could hear him bumping around until he reached the bottom.

"I hope it did not hurt him," Raggedy Ann said. "Listen!"

They could hear the tired old Horse kicking around way down below. And presently they heard his footsteps as he came climbing up.

"Are you there?" the tired old Horse called up through the stone trap-door.

"Yes," Raggedy Ann replied. "What shall we do?"

"I took a peachy tumble," the Horse called back. "If you just press down gently upon the stone, I am sure it will open." And indeed, this proved correct, for when Raggedy Andy pressed down ever so lightly, the stone lowered and they could see the tired old Horse standing upon the stone steps.

"Come on," he said, "I will hold the stone trap-door open until you all get in. But watch you don't slip on the stone steps, for it is a long way to the bottom."

"That ring was just put in the top of the stone to fool anyone who came into the tree," Raggedy Andy said when all had safely reached the bottom of the stone steps. "For the ring made it look as though you had to pull on the trap-door to open it."

"I am glad that it was I who sat upon the stone instead of Jenny," the tired old Horse laughed.

CHAPTER FIVE

A WONDERFUL sight met their eyes, when the tired old Horse opened a door at the bottom of the stone steps and our friends walked out into the open again. There, in the distance, upon a wonderful hill, stood a beautiful castle with turrets and spires of red reaching up towards the sky. And between our friends and the castle, there was a large valley filled with strangely-shaped little houses. From where they stood, Raggedy Ann and Raggedy Andy, Jenny, the tired old Horse and the Camel with the wrinkled knees could see the Loonies running about in the streets like mad. First running one way and then running another.

"What's the matter with them, I wonder?" the tired old Horse said. Of course neither Jenny or any of her friends knew the reason, so they could not answer. But soon the Loonies all came running towards them shouting and waving sticks.

"I believe that they see us," said the Camel, who had removed the blindfold from his eyes.

This was true, for the queer little Loonies came swarming towards them, looking for all the world like ants as they crossed the valley.

"Where can we hide?" Jenny asked, as she looked about her.

"We shan't hide!" Raggedy Andy cried. "We will wait and see what they intend doing."

The Loonies soon showed our friends what they intended doing, for they all surrounded Raggedy Ann and Jenny and Raggedy Andy and the tired old Horse and the Camel with the wrinkled knees, and poking them with their sticks, started marching our friends down into the valley towards the queer houses.

"Do you think it would be a good plan for me to start

©
JOHNNY GRUELLE

kicking?" the tired old Horse whispered to Raggedy Ann. "I can knock them head-over-heels if I start kicking and thrashing about."

"I do not believe I would do that," Raggedy Ann replied. "For your heels are hard and you would hurt them very much should you kick any of the Loonies."

"All right," the tired old Horse agreed. "Then we will march along quietly."

The Loonies marched their prisoners into the largest house in the center of all the other queer houses and up before the King of the Loonies.

"Aha!" the Loonie King cried, when all the Loonies had stopped their chattering. "What have we captured?"

One of the Loonies who had captured our friends spoke and said to the Loonie King, "Oh, most Looniest of Loonies, we have captured those who came down through the great tree."

"Don't I know that?" the Loonie King howled. "Why don't you answer my question? Whom have we captured?"

"We have captured the prisoners," the Loonie Guard replied.

"Good!" the Loonie King cried, as he clapped his hands. "Now see if you can answer this one. What will we do with them now that we have captured them?"

"Put them in prison, I guess," the Guard replied.

"Wrong!" shouted the Loonie King. "Now try to think!"

"I can't seem to think of anything," the Guard answered.

"Good!" the Loonie King again clapped his hands together. "You guessed that I was thinking that I couldn't think of anything either! Now here is another and this is the hardest of all. What is the name of that man with the funny hat?" And the Loonie King pointed his long finger at the Horse.

The tired old Horse looked around at his friends and winked one eye. "He called me a man," he giggled.

"Please remain quiet when I am asking riddles!" the Loonie King shouted at the Horse.

"His name is Spoogledoogle," the Guard said.

"Good!" the Loonie King again cried as he clapped his hands. "That is right."

"It is wrong," the tired old Horse said.

"It is right!" the Loonie King cried. "Whatever I say is right, *is* right, whether it is right or wrong!"

"All right," the tired old Horse replied. "I shall not argue with you, but I know that I am not a Spoogledoogle, for there isn't any such animal!" And with this, the tired old Horse walked over and laid down in a small flower garden at one side of the room.

"Here!" the Loonie King shouted at the tired old Horse. "Get out of that flower bed! You are worse than the neighbor's chickens!" The tired old Horse made no reply, but put his head down upon the prettiest flowers and went to sleep. The Loonie King took off his crown and scratched his head. "Do all Spoogledoogles act that way?" he finally asked Raggedy Ann.

"Oh yes," Raggedy Ann replied, with a twinkle in her shoe-button eyes. "If you watch him for awhile, you will see that when he gets up he will be a Horse instead of a Spoogledoogle." And Jenny and Raggedy Andy snickered behind their hands.

The Loonie King looked doubtfully at Raggedy Ann. "Why did you come to The Loonie Land?" he asked.

"We came in search of Jan," Raggedy Ann replied, "One of the Loonies carried him away from his sister, and we are searching for him."

"Hmm!" the Loonie King mused as he rubbed his chin. "Now I must try and fool you. My Loonie did not catch Jan near the little cottage in the deep, deep woods and drag him down here."

"Oh!" Raggedy Ann cried as she put her hands to her face. "What a fib!"

"How do you know it's a fib?" the Loonie King asked.

"Because," Raggedy Ann replied. "If the Loonie did not do that, how do you know he caught Jan near the little cottage in the deep, deep woods?"

"That's so," the Loonie King agreed. "Well, anyway, it doesn't make any difference. Jan is in prison, and if you want him, you must answer three riddles."

"Do you mean that if we answer the three riddles, you will let Jan go with us?" Raggedy Andy asked the Loonie King.

"Yes," the King replied. Then he told one of the Guards to bring Jan into the room. When the Guard returned with Jan, the Loonie King said, "Now I shall ask the three riddles."

"Let's see," he mused, "Why does a boliver bite biscuits? There's a hard one."

"I don't believe it is a riddle at all!" Jenny whispered to Raggedy Ann. "He's just making it up."

"I think so too," Raggedy Ann replied.

"What are you talking about?" the Loonie King asked.

"The boliver bites biscuits because he wishes to eat them," Raggedy Ann told the Loonie King.

"Good!" the King cried, "I mean, bad, for I do not wish you to guess them. Now! Why does a snickersnapper snap snickers from snuckers?"

"Isn't that silly?" the Camel with the wrinkled knees laughed.

"Don't you think that is a good one?" the King asked the Camel.

"Indeed, I do!" the Camel replied, "That is the Looniest one you have asked so far."

"I think so, too," the King replied proudly. "Now just you answer that one if you can. Just you answer that one!" he said to Raggedy Ann.

"The snickersnapper snaps snickers from snuckers because the snappersnicker snucks snickersnuckers from snuckersnappers snickersnappers," Raggedy Ann replied, and it was all she could do to keep from laughing out loud. Raggedy Andy could not help it, he laughed so hard he fell upon the floor and rolled about.

"I don't see how you guess them so easily!" the Loonie King cried, "I never would be able to guess them myself!"

Of course, Raggedy Ann did not tell the Loonie King that she did not know the answers herself, for she knew that the Loonie King did not know the answers either, for he just made up the riddles as he went along.

"Now I have thought of a real, real hard one," the Loonie King said. "How can a hobgoblin hobble a gobble? Guess that riddle and I'll give you a fiddle."

"Anything you answer will be right," Jenny whispered. "The Loonie King does not know the answers himself."

"I know it," Raggedy Ann replied out loud.

"Then if you know it, why don't you answer?" the Loonie King cried.

"The hobgoblin can hobble a gobble by gobbling the hobble with a goghobblin," Raggedy Ann answered.

"Good!" the Loonie King cried, then remembering that he had not wanted Raggedy Ann to answer correctly, he shrieked, "No, I mean BAD! I did not wish you to guess my riddles so easily! Now I will have to ask you some more!"

"Oh, that isn't fair," Raggedy Ann said. "You promised if I answered three riddles, you would let Jan go away with us, so it wouldn't be fair if you did not keep your promise!"

"I've changed my mind now," the Loonie King replied. "I shall ask you three more riddles; then if you answer them correctly, I will let you take Jan."

"No, sir!" Raggedy Ann replied. "You said three in the beginning. And I answered the three riddles. How do I know but what you might change your mind after I answered the next three?"

"Of course, you wouldn't know," the Loonie King said, "But that is just what I would do! I have a right to change my mind every time I feel like it, I guess!"

©
JOHNNY GRUELLE

"Well, anyway," Raggedy Andy walked up to the King· "Raggedy Ann answered the riddles, so now we shall take Jan and leave you," he said.

"Ha! Ha! Is that so?" the King howled. "I shall see that you do not escape! Bring out the Looniest Knight I have. I shall have him cut off your nose!"

"Boo! Boo!" Raggedy Andy howled back at the King as loud as the King had howled at Raggedy Andy. Then the Loonie King stuck out his tongue at Raggedy Andy and before he thought what he was doing Raggedy Andy tweeked the King's nose so hard it made two large tears run out of the King's eyes.

Just then the Looniest Knight came galloping in, sitting astride a stick with a horse's head on the end. The Looniest Knight pranced up before the King and waved his sword, "Whose nose is it, the Looniest King wishes cut off?" the Knight asked.

"There he is!" shouted the Loonie King, pointing to Raggedy Andy. The Looniest Knight rushed at Raggedy Andy and would have tried to cut off Raggedy Andy's nose if Raggedy Andy had not hurriedly crossed his fingers. The Looniest Knight did not know what to do when Raggedy Andy crossed his fingers, for you know, and of course everyone else knows, that means "King's Ex."

"What shall I do?" the Looniest Knight asked the King

"You must fight!" the King cried. "Didn't you see him tweek my nose?"

"No, I didn't!" the Looniest Knight replied. "How did he do it?"

"Like this," Raggedy Andy laughed, as he tweeked the Looniest Knight's nose. Then while the Looniest Knight was wiping the tears from his eyes, Raggedy Andy awakened the tired old Horse and got upon his back. Then taking a long stick away from a Loonie man standing near, Raggedy Andy uncrossed his fingers. This was a sign that he was ready to fight.

Then the Looniest Knight jumped around with his hobby horse just as if he was on a real horse which was prancing about as if he could not guide it the way he wanted it to go.

"I believe he is afraid," Raggedy Andy laughed.

"He isn't afraid," the Loonie King said, "he just doesn't want to fight until he gets ready."

But although Raggedy Andy waited patiently, the Looniest Knight kept on prancing about just as if he could not make his hobby horse behave. Then finally, the Looniest Knight dropped his sword upon the floor and kicked up his heels and pretended that his hobby horse threw him.

"That wasn't any fight at all!" the Camel with the wrinkled knees cried. "The Looniest Knight was afraid of Raggedy Andy! That's what!"

"Sometimes he fights better than that," the Loonie King said. "Maybe he was afraid that Raggedy Andy would crack him with the long stick."

"Of course, I meant to crack him," Raggedy Andy laughed. "And I'll crack anyone who tries to keep Jan from going with us."

At this all the Loonies cheered loudly and the Loonie King came down from his throne and shook Raggedy Andy's hand. Then he shook hands with the tired old Horse who had gone to sleep standing up. Then he shook hands with Jenny and Jan and Raggedy Ann and the Camel with the wrinkled knees.

"You are so brave, I wouldn't think of keeping Jan any longer," the Loonie King told them. "So you can all leave." And as our friends marched out of the Loonie King's house with Jan, all the Loonies ran after them shouting, "Long live the brave Raggedy Andy! He vanquished the Looniest Knight!" And even the Looniest Knight and the Loonie King ran with them to the end of the village, shouting with the rest of the Loonies.

"Well," Raggedy Andy sighed when they had left the Loonies behind at the edge of Loonie Town. "I am mighty glad that is over! I never was so frightened in my whole life!"

"Were you really?" Jenny asked. "Why you didn't let on that you were."

"Of course not!" Raggedy Andy laughed. "If I had let them know that I was more frightened than the Looniest Knight, don't you see he wouldn't have been as frightened as I and would have cut off my nose," laughed Raggedy Andy. "And I didn't care to have my nose cut off, because then all my cotton stuffing would have leaked out and my head would have been as flat as a pancake."

"Well, here we are back at the tree," the tired old Horse said.

"Yes," Raggedy Andy added. "And I have been riding you all this time when you are so tired!" And Raggedy Andy jumped from the Horse's back.

"Really, I had not noticed it at all," the Horse laughed.

CHAPTER SIX

"OH, WAIT a minute!" Raggedy Ann said, as they were about to enter the tree. "We do not want to go back up through the tree until we find Babette, the French doll! We must blindfold the Camel with the wrinkled knees and let him run backwards."

"Let's see," the tired old Horse thought out loud, "I will carry Jan and Jenny, while the Camel carries Raggedy Ann and Raggedy Andy. In that way we can get there quicker."

So Raggedy Ann again tied her hanky around the Camel's shoe-button eyes and after she and Raggedy Andy had climbed upon his back and Jan and Jenny upon the tired old Horse's back, the Camel started running backward lickety-split.

The tired old Horse ran just behind the Camel's head and as Raggedy Ann and Raggedy Andy sat facing Jan and Jenny upon the Horse's back, they could talk comfortably as they rode along.

After they had galloped along for ten minutes, the Camel suddenly stopped and as the tired old Horse had been running with his nose very close to the Camel's nose, he bumped into the Camel so hard, the Camel's soft head was pushed way back in wrinkles against his body, and Jan and Jenny went over the Horse's head and landed upon Raggedy Andy and Raggedy Ann.

"It is lucky you fell on us!" Raggedy Ann laughed, as Jan and Jenny got to their feet. "For Raggedy Andy and I are soft and it did not bump you much."

"It did not hurt us a bit!" Jan laughed as he brushed off Raggedy Ann's dress. "But how about the Camel?"

Indeed the Camel with the wrinkled knees did look very sad. His poor nose was flat and his neck was nothing but wrinkles. Jan and Raggedy Andy pulled and patted the Camel's head into shape again and it was not long until he looked as good as before.

© JOHNNY GRUELLE

"Why did we stop?" the tired old Horse asked.

"We ran into something," Raggedy Ann said, "but I can't see a thing." None of the others could see anything either, but when they felt in back of the Camel, they could feel an invisible stone wall. And although Raggedy Ann and Raggedy Andy ran along the wall for a long way, feeling it, they could discover no gate.

"There must be some way of getting in right here!" the Camel said, "for I am certain this is the exact spot I came out of."

"Maybe if you came out here there is a door, or gate there," Jan said.

"And maybe it only opens one way, like the stone at the room in the tree," Raggedy Ann suggested.

"But if that was so, I would have fallen through, just as the tired old Horse did," the Camel said.

"Oh, no you wouldn't," Raggedy Ann laughed. "For don't you see, Mister Camel, if you came out a door there, it must have swung out this way, and if you bump it from this side, it only closes that much tighter."

"That's so," the Camel agreed. "But can you feel any door knob?" Raggedy Ann had to admit that she could not, so there they were and could not get in.

After thinking for a while the tired old Horse finally suggested, "Let the Camel back up tight against the gate; for there must be a gate right here; and Raggedy Ann and Raggedy Andy get upon the Camel's back. Then the Camel can pretend that he has just come bouncing through the invisible gate and start to run. This may fool the gate into thinking the same thing and it may swing open as it would do just as some one passed through it."

"But it will close again," the Camel said. "Then we are just where we started from."

"Yes, but if the invisible gate swings open, I shall hold it open," the tired old Horse said. "Then you can come back and we will all go through."

"It sounds reasonable," Raggedy Andy said, "let's try it, for there is nothing else to do." And he and Raggedy Ann climbed upon the Camel's back and the Camel squeezed back tight against the invisible gate. Then with a sudden spring, the Camel jumped away from the wall and ran a few steps.

"I've got it!" the tired old Horse called as he held the invisible gate open.

"How did you ever think of it?" the Camel asked, as he and the others walked through the invisible gate.

"I don't know," the Horse laughed. "I guess it was just plain Horse sense."

"Well, here we are," Raggedy Ann said, when they had all passed through the invisible gate. "And there is a queer little house built of sticks and stones and mud over there."

"I'll go over and see who lives there," Raggedy Andy said.

"We'd better all go," Raggedy Ann suggested. And so they all walked over to the queer little house. As they stood looking at it, a little old woman peeped slyly out of a crack in the door, then the door was opened wide and the little old woman came out. "Good morning," she said, "Can I serve you with any Witch-craft today?"

"I've never tasted any," the tired old Horse replied. "But if it is anything which will keep me from getting so tired, I'd like to eat some."

"She doesn't mean food, Mister Horse, when she says Witch-craft," Raggedy Ann explained. "She means Magic!"

"Yes, that is just what I mean," the little old woman said. "I'm Winnie the Witch, and I serve people with Witch-craft. It is very cheap."

"How much is a nickel's worth?" the tired old Horse asked.

"Just five cents," Winnie the Witch replied. "What kind would you like to have, kind sir?"

The tired old Horse fumbled in his pocket and finally found a nickel and handed it to the Witch. "I'll take any kind you have, just so it is good for being tired," he said.

"Something in the shape of a bicycle pump?" the Witch inquired.

"He isn't an automobile," Raggedy Ann laughed. "What he wants is some hay, or oats, or corn that has been Magically made Magic to cure him of being tired."

"Yes, that is what I want," the tired old Horse agreed. "I don't care what it is, just so it makes me want to move quickly."

The Witch bit the nickel, then tinkled it upon her door step. "I just want to make sure it isn't lead," she said. "Yesterday a man came here with the loveliest doll and gave me ten cents for a bottle of Magic Medicine to make the doll come to life."

"It must have been the French doll, Babette!" Raggedy Ann and Raggedy Andy cried together. "And did you give him the Magic Medicine?" Raggedy Ann asked.

"Oh, yes," the Witch said. "But after he left, I tinkled the ten cent piece on the table and it was lead."

"He cheated you!" cried Raggedy Ann.

"Indeed, he cheated himself," laughed the Witch. "For whenever anyone tries to cheat me, whatever I sell them never does what they wish it to do. And so, you see, the bottle of Magic Medicine which I gave him turned to plain, everyday water just as soon as he gave me the lead dime."

The Witch, when she had finished telling our friend this, said, "Now we must all remain very quiet, while I work the magic charm for the tired old Horse." Then from her pocket she took a piece of red chalk and made a ring upon the ground. In the ring she drew many strange figures, each with a number beside it. Then she asked the Horse to step into the circle and shut his eyes. When he had done this, the Witch took a stick and gave the tired old Horse a crack upon his back. "Giddap!" she cried. And the tired old Horse jumped out of the circle and went scampering about with his head high in the air.

"There," the Witch said, with a sly wink at Raggedy Ann. "That was all he needed! In fact, anyone who is always tired needs the same thing, for they just imagine they are tired." Then when the tired old Horse came prancing back to his friends, he was so pleased he wanted all the rest to have some Magic too.

"I'm not a bit tired now," the Horse said. "I could carry all of you upon my back a long way now and not be the least bit tired! I could feel the Magic strike me all of a sudden," he told the Witch. "It was wonderful!"

"I haven't any nickels, or dimes," Raggedy Ann told the Witch. "But I wish that you could tell us how to find the man who had the doll. For we are in search of her and would like very much to find her and take her back home with us."

"I'll tell you a secret," the Witch whispered, after first looking all about her to make sure there was no one listening. "I do not care whether anyone pays me for working magic, or not. So," she went on out loud, "I will see what I can do for you. Please step into the Magic Circle, all of you."

"Shall we receive the same sort of Magic that the tired old Horse received?" Jan asked. "I wouldn't care to have Jenny get it."

"Now please do not worry about that," the Witch promised. "You will not feel anything at all." Then when they had all stepped into the Magic Circle the Witch said, "You must all close your eyes and count ten slowly. Then you may open your eyes."

Raggedy Ann, Raggedy Andy, Jan and Jenny, the tired old Horse and the Camel with the wrinkled knees all counted slowly to ten, then opened their eyes. Instead of the little house belonging to the Witch, which had stood a few feet from them before, our friends saw a large tent and coming from the tent were voices. Very quietly they walked up to the side of the tent and listened.

"Ha!" one voice said, "The old Witch cheated me! The bottle of Magic was nothing but a bottle of rain-water! I shall go back and tear down her house!"

Raggedy Ann found a small hole in the side of the tent and peeped through, then she motioned the others to take a peep. There, sitting inside were twelve large men with black whiskers and long red noses. And each one had a large sword and two pistols in his belt.

"They are Pirates or something, I'll bet," Raggedy Andy whispered. "And there is Babette pretending she was only a doll and not moving at all! What shall we do? We must rescue Babette some way, but the Pirates are too large to fight!"

"They look very fierce," Jenny said. "Perhaps they will capture us all and keep us prisoners."

"Listen," Raggedy Ann whispered. "They are talking."

"Ha!" laughed one of the Pirates. "I am about the bravest Pirate around here!"

"We are all of us the bravest!" all the other Pirates cried, each trying to say it louder than the others.

"How can we all be the bravest, I'd like to know?" the first Pirate asked.

"Because," one replied. "We are really not Pirates at all! So we all can be as brave Pirates as another!"

"That is quite true!" all the Pirates agreed, except the first one, and he seemed to be the Chief. "How can you prove that you are as brave as I am?" he asked.

"I know how we can prove which is the bravest!" one thin Pirate cried. "We can take twelve pieces of paper and put a spot on one piece, then we can put all the pieces of paper in the hat and draw. The one who draws the black spot can be shot by the rest of us. Then we'll put eleven pieces of paper in with one having a black spot and keep on until there is only one left and that will be me!"

"How can it be you?" the others all asked.

"Because I will mark the paper and remember which one it is each time," the thin Pirate said.

"I shall be the one to mark the black spot!" the other

eleven Pirates cried. "For I want to be the last one left alive!"

"They'll be fighting in a few minutes," Raggedy Andy whispered, although it was not necessary for him to be quiet, the Pirates were quarrelling so loud they would not have heard had Raggedy Andy shouted.

Jan took a tin tube from his pocket and picked up some small pebbles, then whispering for his friends to keep still,

he went around the tent until he found a small hole near one of the Pirates. Then with his tin tube Jan blew a pebble against a Pirate's cheek.

"Wow!" the Pirate howled as he jumped up and danced about. "Who hit me?" Then Jan blew pebbles against the other Pirates' cheeks until they were all dancing about,

howling. Jan could scarcely blow the pebbles at the Pirates, he was laughing so hard, but when he could manage to straighten his face, he stung them with the pebbles. Then, not knowing what was happening to them, the Pirates all decided that it was safer outside the tent. And, each trying to get there first caused a jam at the doorway, and in a tangle of arms, legs and heads the Pirates fell in a struggling mass, pulling the tent down with them.

Jan immediately reached under the fallen tent, picked up Babette and carried her to where Jenny, Raggedy Ann, the tired old Horse and the Camel with the wrinkled knees stood with Raggedy Andy.

The Pirates were struggling to their feet and there was no time to be lost. "Quick!" the tired old Horse cried, "Jan and Jenny upon my back and Raggedy Ann, Babette and Raggedy Andy upon the Camel's back."

This was done, just as the first Pirate got to his feet. And, seeing our friends running away, he knew in a moment what had happened.

With a loud shout to his companions, the Pirate started running after our friends. And as the other pirates got to their feet, they followed. Then, as the tired old Horse and the Camel with the wrinkled knees could run very fast, the Pirates began shooting. Luckily, none of the Pirates knew how to shoot straight, so in a short time the Camel and the tired old Horse had left the Pirates far behind.

CHAPTER SEVEN

AFTER the tired old Horse and the Camel with the wrinkled knees had run for a long, long time, they sat down to rest, and as they did not tell their riders what they intended doing, Raggedy Ann, Raggedy Andy, Babette, Jenny and Jan slid right off onto the ground.

"I forgot to mention that I intended sitting down," the tired old Horse said.

"So did I," the Camel chimed in. "It's funny how I just took a sudden notion to stop and rest just as the tired old Horse did."

"Well, no one was hurt," Raggedy Ann laughed, "So please do not appologize."

"Babette is a lovely doll, isn't she?" Jenny said as she smoothed the French doll's hair.

"Indeed she is," Raggedy Ann and Raggedy Andy both agreed. "She's the prettiest doll of all."

"It's nice to have you say that, Raggedy Ann and Raggedy Andy!" Babette smiled so that her dimples showed. "But really, I must tell you that Raggedy Ann is the most beloved doll of all, isn't she, Raggedy Andy?"

"Yes, indeed that is true," Raggedy Andy told Jenny. "You see, Raggedy Ann is so old and so loppy and so generous and so kindly, and she can think so much better than any of us other dolls. And then, too," Raggedy Andy said, "Maybe you don't know it, but Raggedy Ann has a candy heart! Haven't you, Raggedy Ann?"

"Honest?" asked the Camel with the wrinkled knees. "Let's see it."

"Oh, it is sewed up inside my cotton-stuffed body," Raggedy Ann laughed.

"I thought maybe you had it in your apron pocket," the Camel said.

"Here, look," Raggedy Andy told the Camel. "You

© JOHNNY GRUELLE

can feel Raggedy Ann's candy heart." And Raggedy Andy showed the other just where to feel. Even the tired old Horse was greatly surprised when he felt such a lovely candy heart.

"Were you frightened when the Pirate took you out of the playroom, Babette?" Raggedy Andy asked.

"Not a bit," Babette replied. "Only of course I did not wish to be taken away and I was afraid the Pirate would drop me and break my china head when he jumped over the fence."

"I thought you were a French doll," the Camel cried.

"She is," Raggedy Andy told the Camel. "What makes you think she isn't, Mister?"

"Because," the Camel said, as he scratched his head as

if trying to figure it all out. "If she has a China head, she must be Chinese, so she can't be French." Everyone laughed at this and the tired old Horse turned a summersault and kicked up his heels with glee.

The Camel sat with a puzzled expression on his canton flannel face. "Well," he cried, "Just you tell me then. How can she be French when she is Chinese? Just you tell me that."

"How can a brick walk?" the Horse laughed. "Or a housefly?"

"I shan't answer your riddles unless you answer mine." the Camel said.

"Then I'll explain," the Horse started to say, when he saw in the distance a strange object bobbing up and down the ground and coming towards them. "Look!" he cried.

"It's a housefly!" the Camel cried, "I mean it's a flying house!"

"Indeed it is," Babette jumped to her feet, "It is the jumping houseboat of the Pirates! Run as fast as you can!"

The Camel with the wrinkled knees immediately started running and the tired old Horse had to run after him and drag him back to the others by the string the Camel had for a tail.

"Now just see the time you've made us waste!" the tired old Horse shouted. "You know perfectly well that you and I must carry the others! Quick!" he cried. "Climb upon our backs!"

The Camel with the wrinkled knees couldn't think of anything to reply until he and the tired old Horse had run almost a mile, then he cried to the horse, "Wait a minute! I just thought of something I want to tell you!"

"Tell me as we run along," the tired old Horse shouted back at the Camel. "Can't you see the Pirates are gaining on us every minute?"

"I just wanted to tell you not to be so bossy, MisterTired Old Horse!" the Camel puffed as his black shoe-button eyes sparkled.

"Please do not stop to quarrel," Raggedy Ann said. "There is the Witch's little house right ahead."

"Shall we dash right in without knocking?" the Camel asked as he ran faster.

"Of course not," the tired old Horse replied as he also ran faster. "If the door is closed and we dash in, we would only break the door down and then the Pirates could dash in after us."

"The Pirates are right behind us," Jan shouted. "Hurry!"

Indeed, the Pirates' jumping houseboat was jumping right behind them when the Witch opened her front door and cried, "Run right in!"

The tired old Horse was the first in the door and the Camel with the wrinkled knees was right behind him. And they both came into the Witch's house so fast and it was such a small place inside, neither could stop although they braced their feet in front of themselves. The tired old Horse, Jenny and Jan, the Camel with the wrinkled knees, Raggedy Ann, Raggedy Andy and Babette slid across the floor and upset a large bowl of gold fish.

The witch slammed the door, "BANG!" right in the Pirate Chief's face, and the Camel cried excitedly, "I'm shot!"

Jenny and Jan picked up the bowl and replaced the gold-fish before they had flopped very much, and the Witch ran to the kitchen and brought a pail of water to refill the bowl. By this time everyone had got on his feet except the tired old Horse, who had fallen in such a comfortable position he had gone to sleep.

The Pirate Chief banged upon the Witch's door with his sword. "Open the door, or I'll huff and I'll puff and I'll blow the house in!"

"Ha! Ha!" Raggedy Ann and Raggedy Andy laughed. "He has read that in a book! He can't huff and puff enough to blow the house in!"

"I'll soon show you!" the Pirate Chief howled. "You do not know what a good blower I am!" And he puffed so hard his eyes stuck out and it made him dizzy, but still he huffed and puffed! Then after huffing and puffing for six minutes, the Pirate Chief started coughing so hard the other Pirates had to pound him on the back. All those inside the Witch's house had been peeping through the chinks in the window-blinds, and when the Pirate Chief had to give up his huffing and puffing Raggedy Ann and her friends laughed real loud and long.

"I know what we will do," the Pirate Chief said, after he had quit coughing.

"What will we do?" the others asked, as they crowded about him.

"We will lay a siege and starve them out! I've read in a book about how Kings often lay siege to a castle until the inmates are starved out!"

"But where will we get the siege to lay?" one Pirate asked.

"And beside!" another cried. "This isn't a castle!"

"Sillies!" the Chief cried, as he stamped around. "That doesn't make a bit of difference! All we have to do is to stay here until they get so hungry they come out and beg for something to eat!"

"That sounds like a good scheme," the thinnest Pirate admitted. "But won't we be getting just as hungry as they?"

"Of course not," the Pirate Chief replied. "We have a lot of things to eat in the jumping houseboat. And if we bring the food out here and eat it, that will make them hungry and very soon they will come out."

Now as everyone knows, Pirates are always very, very hungry. In fact almost as hungry as little boys, so they all ran to the flying boat and came out carrying bread and butter and dill pickles.

"Look!" the Pirates yelled to those in the Witch's house. "We've got something to eat! Yaha! Yaha!"

"That reminds me," the tired old Horse said as he got up and yawned. "I haven't had a bite to eat since I ate the violets."

"Snap Dragons," the Camel corrected.

"Violets," the tired old Horse replied very firmly.

"Yaha! Yaha! We've got bread and butter and dill pickles!" the Pirates teased outside.

"We don't care! We don't care!" Jan and Jenny called back.

"And we've got some sugar to put on our bread and butter, too, if we want it!" the Pirates yelled. "Yaha! Yaha! And you haven't!"

"Here we are," the Witch said; for, while the others had been watching out the cracks with hungry eyes, she prepared a lovely lunch with her magic charms. There were ham sandwiches, bread and butter and jelly sandwiches, pickles, ice cream, lady-fingers, doughnuts and watermelon. Everything looked so good it made tears come in Raggedy Ann's, Raggedy Andy's and the Camel's shoe-button eyes, for they had no mouths to eat with. And when the Witch noticed this, she took a pair of little scissors and snipped a mouth for each. Jenny and Jan and the tired old Horse, of course, were already sitting at the table with napkins

© JOHNNY GRUELLE

tucked under their chins. All the time our friends were eating the lovely magical lunch the Witch had prepared for them, the Pirates were sitting outside with only bread and butter and dill pickles.

When everyone had eaten all they could, the tired old Horse said, "While you rest, for I know you are all sleepy from eating so much, I will 'red up' the table and wash the dishes." So the Witch, who was as sleepy as the rest, placed pillows around upon the floor and everyone laid down and took a nap. The Horse took all the cream puffs and ladyfingers and ham sandwiches that had been left on the plates to a side window and threw them out.

"Kittie! Kittie! Kittie!" he called and laughed softly to himself. All the Pirates came running to see what the tired old Horse had thrown out the window. "Are your names all Kittie?" the tired old Horse asked.

The Pirates saw all the nice things the horse had thrown out the window and said to each other. "Just look at the goodies they have thrown away, cream puffs and ladyfingers and ham sandwiches and *watermelon!* My goodness! They must have a lot of good things to eat if they can throw away these nice things!

"And all we had was bread and butter and dill pickles!" And the Pirates all had tears in their eyes and mouths, for as you must surely know, the tired old Horse had made them very, very hungry.

"We had the nicest lunch you ever, ever saw," the tired old Horse told the Pirates. "And if you promise to behave yourselves, I'll give you each a lollypop for I did not throw them away!"

"I'll promise," all the Pirates shouted, as they crowded about the window with outstretched hands.

The tired old Horse held out twelve lollypops. "Now if I give you each a lollypop you must promise to reform and not be Pirates any more. Now what will you be if you quit

being Pirates?" The tired old Horse held the lollypops so high the Pirates could not reach them.

"I'll quit being a Pirate and be a plumber!" one Pirate cried.

"And I'll quit being a Pirate and go in the garage business!" another shouted.

"And I'll quit being a Pirate and sell oil stock!" another cried.

"And I'll quit being a Pirate and be a—"

"Wait a minute!" the tired old Horse laughed, as he scratched his head. "I believe you had all better remain Pirates! So promise me you will be Pirates instead of driving taxi cabs, or going into the plumbing business or anything like that!"

When the Pirates had all said, "Cross my heart!" and promised, the tired old Horse gave them each a lollypop. Then one of the Pirates began crying and handed his lollypop back to the tired old Horse. "What's the matter?" the tired old Horse asked, "Isn't your lollypop as large as the others?"

"Yes! Snub! Snub!" the Pirate sobbed. "But it makes me feel sorry that I took the doll away from its home. And I am ashamed to have you be so kind to me after I was so naughty." And the Pirate cried and cried as if his heart would break. In fact, he cried so hard, he got all the other Pirates to crying and they cried so hard, they could not eat their lollypops.

If it had not been so sad, the tired old Horse would have laughed, for the Pirates were all squawling in different keys and it sounded very strange.

"What is all the racket about?" the Witch asked, as she

and the others came to the windows. "Did you put red pepper on the lollypops?"

"No," the tired old Horse replied, as he brushed away a tear and told his friends why the Pirates wept so loudly.

"I'll bet a nickel they have reformed," the Witch said.

"It isn't that," one of the Pirates said. "Charlie here is crying because he took the French Doll, and he knows that was very, very wrong. And the rest of us are crying to think that one of our band would be so dishonest."

"Gracious!" the Camel with the wrinkled knees said. "I thought all Pirates were dishonest."

"Maybe they are," the Pirate Chief replied. "But you see, we were really not real-for-sure Pirates. We were just pretending that we were Pirates and that is why we all feel so sad about Charlie."

"And I feel sadder and sadder and sadder and sadder every minute," the Pirate named Charlie howled.

Raggedy Ann felt so sorry for Charlie and the other Pirates, she went outside and wiped Charlie's tears away with her apron. "Now please do not cry any more, Pirate Charlie," Raggedy Ann said as she gave him a large fluffy cream puff with lots of cream in it. "We will forgive you for taking Babette and we know you will never do anything like that again."

Pirate Charlie smiled through his tears as he ate the lovely cream puff. "I'll tell you, Raggedy Ann," Pirate Charlie said, after Raggedy Ann had wiped the cream from around his mouth with her pocket hanky. "We always read stories about Pirates when we were little, and all of us decided that when we grew up we would become Pirates and sail through the air in a big flying houseboat. So when we finally grew up, we bought this jumping boat and pretended that we were Pirates. But all the time we longed for the things we should have had when we were children. And I always wanted a lovely doll. That is why I took the French doll."

By this time Raggedy Andy, the tired old Horse, Jenny and Jan and the others had gathered around the Pirates as they sat on the grass by the side of the Witch's little house. The kindly Witch brought out large dishes of ice cream for everyone and stood looking at the Pirates intently for a few minutes.

When everyone had finished eating their ice cream, the Witch, with a tinkly little laugh, said, "I want all the Pirates to sit in this circle!" And she drew a circle upon the ground. When the Pirates had all taken seats inside the circle, the Witch placed a small red thing in the center of the circle and leading from the small red thing to the outside of the circle was a small rubber tube.

After the Witch had said a magic charm like this—"Hi Diddle Diddle, the Cat and the Fiddle!" only she said it backwards, she placed the small rubber tube in her mouth and started blowing. And, as the Witch blew, everyone saw that the small red thing was a red balloon, and it grew larger and larger until it was almost touching the Pirates' knees. Then the red balloon burst with a loud "Bang!" and everyone except the Witch was so surprised they fell over backward.

"Why!" the Camel with the wrinkled knees cried, when he got to his feet and looked at the Pirates. "They have had a magic shave!" Indeed, all the Pirates had lost their black whiskers and long red noses.

"They are all GIRLS!" Jan and Jenny cried in astonishment. The magic red balloon had blown the Pirates' false whiskers and false noses right off their faces. "Now girls," the Witch laughed, "You had better all come in my house and wash the red paint from your faces."

©
JOHNNY GRUELLE

CHAPTER EIGHT

IT IS remarkable how black whiskers and false noses and red paint will change anyone's appearance. For, after the Pirates had had their false whiskers and false noses blown off and had washed the red paint from their faces, they were all pretty girls.

"We even changed our names," the Pirate who had been called Charlie said. "My name is Charlotte."

The Witch picked up all the false whiskers and long red false noses and took them to the Pirate jumping boat. "Everybody climb on board," she said. "For we will ask the Girl Pirates to take us in the jumping boat to find Jan and Jenny's mother and father."

"Why, how do you know about their mother, Mrs. Witch?" the tired old Horse asked in surprise.

The Witch just laughed a tinkly laugh and took off her large hat. And with the hat came all her white straggly hair. Then she took off her long black cloak and stood before them a lovely girl not any older-looking than Jenny.

"Land sakes alive!" the Camel with the wrinkled knees cried. "She isn't a Witch at all! She's a Fairy Queen!" Everyone else was as much astonished as the Camel with the wrinkled knees.

"No," the Fairy who had been a Witch a moment before said. "I am not a Fairy Queen. I am only a Fairy Princess." And as the Fairy Princess waved her magic wand again the Girl Pirates' jumping houseboat became covered with beautiful fairy lights and started jumping along over the ground. It was just like sailing along over the water when the sea causes the boat to rise and fall with a gentle motion, and everyone enjoyed riding upon the Pirates' jumping boat.

"I thought it was funny that a Witch could be as kindly as you were," the tired old Horse said to the Fairy Princess.

"But one really can never tell by appearances," Raggedy Andy said.

"That is indeed true," the Fairy Princess laughed. "But so many persons always judge people by the way in which they are dressed. Why, the ugliest shell may be hiding the most beautiful pearl and the roughest cover may be on the loveliest, sweetest story book. It isn't what is on the outside that counts; it is what we may have within us. But," the Fairy Princess laughed. "We must not conceal our good qualities, but must let others share them with us, for, whenever we give, then we most surely receive in return. And indeed, a heart filled with love within us always shines through in the kindly acts we do and in the sunshine we give to others."

The jumping boat had now reached the Land of the Loonies and jumped around their queer village towards the beautiful castle which stood upon the purple mountain beyond.

"Are we going to the lovely castle?" Jenny asked the Princess.

"Yes, my dear," the Fairy Princess replied. "For there we shall find your mother and father. And while we are sailing there I shall tell you their story. When they left you and Jan," the Princess said as she put her arm around

Jenny, "they went to see your grandmother, and they intended coming back to you in two hours. But when they reached your grandmother's house, they found a lot of knights and courtiers; and indeed, they were very much surprised to find so many fine people there. And when the knights and courtiers saw your mother and father, they all fell upon their knees and cried, 'Long live the King! Long live the Queen!' And your father and mother discovered for the first time that your grandmother had been a queen, but her place had been taken by another woman whose soldiers had driven your grandmother away from the country. Now the other woman who had taken your grandmother's crown had been driven away by the knights who loved your granny and they had come to make her queen again. But Granny had been taken to Fairyland as the knights found when they came to Granny's little house, and they were just about to leave when along came your father and mother. So there wasn't anything to do except go with the knights and courtiers and be crowned King and Queen of the Purple Mountain."

"But why didn't Mother and Daddy send for us?" Jenny asked.

"That is the sad part of the story," the Fairy Princess replied. "You see, everyone thinks it is just lovely to be a King, or a Queen, for then, they imagine they can do just as they please and have everything they wish. But this is not always true. When your father and mother wished to return to their own little home, they found that they were not permitted to do so. For they were never permitted to step outside of the castle unless knights and courtiers went with them. Nor could they send anyone to bring you two children to them! And that is why I am helping you reach your mamma and daddy, for I know how they have longed for you!"

© JOHNNY GRUELLE

The Fairy Princess directed the jumping boat so that it came to rest in a beautiful garden of the lovely castle. And there sat Jenny's and Jan's mamma and daddy, the Queen and King of the Purple Mountain. Jenny and Jan, with whoops of joy ran and threw their arms about their parents. All the Pirate Girls and even the tired old Horse cried with happiness at the meeting.

"We shall get right in the jumping boat and leave with you," the King and Queen told the Fairy Princess. "For we never, never, never care to be a King or a Queen again! The people here, if they wish, can have a republic, like the United States of America; but we would rather be just plain, everyday folks in a plain, everyday house with plain, everyday people for friends!"

And so, the King wrote a note and pinned it to the

chair, telling all the people of the Purple Mountain that he did not wish to be King any longer and that they might crown another King and Queen, or elect a President. Then the jumping boat jumped over the garden wall and sped away until the Purple Mountain and the beautiful castle looked like a little toy far behind. The Fairy Princess served ice cream and chocolate cake to everyone on board, for she knew just how hungry they would all be after so much joy and excitement. So, with laughing and singing a board, the jumping boat finally reached the poor little house of Jenny's father and mother.

"Won't you all come in?" Jenny's mother asked. "The first thing I shall do after I take off my Queen's dress and jewels and get into a plain, everyday dress will be to make a whole lot of pancakes!"

"Whoopee!" the former King cried as he threw his crown up against the woodshed. "And I'll run out and chop a lot of wood to build the fire! I haven't had a chance to chop wood since I was King!"

"I do believe the neighbors have taken care of the chickens all the time we were King and Queen!" the mother laughed. "Bring in a handfull of eggs, Henry," she called to the former King as he stopped chopping wood to moisten the palms of his hands.

"Gee! It sounds good to hear you call me Henry!" the king shouted. "I wouldn't be a King again for all the golden nickels in the world, Harriet!"

After Jenny's mamma had fried pancakes until they were stacked upon the table three feet high, and all the pancakes had disappeared, the Pirate Girls told Raggedy Ann and Raggedy Andy and Babette that they would be glad to take them home in the flying boat.

"I really believe we had better be getting back," Raggedy Ann said, as she wiped her shoe-button eyes with the corner of her apron.

"Please wipe mine too," Raggedy Andy said. "I am sorry to leave such good friends, but what will Marcella think when she discovers that Raggedy Ann, Babette and I are not at home? She will think that we have been stolen."

"I can fix that all right," the Fairy Princess laughed. "I will show you when you get home."

The Camel with the wrinkled knees scratched his head a while and then said, "I have just thought it all over and I believe that the little boy who used to play with me has by this time grown up into a man, and he wouldn't care to play with me again, so I shall adopt Jan for my new master."

When the Camel with the wrinkled knees said this, Jan's father rubbed his eyes and picked up the Camel. As he turned the Camel over and over in his hands and wiggled the Camel's wrinkled knees, he cried, "Why, I believe, Harriet, this is a toy I owned when I was a little boy!" And so it proved to be, when he and the Camel told of different things that had happened years before. "Indeed, you shall adopt Jan!" the former king cried as he gave the Camel a fond squeeze. "And the tired old Horse can adopt us too, if he wishes!"

"Indeed he can!" the former Queen cried. "And we will be most happy to have such a good friend!"

The tired old Horse tried to thank them all, but his throat seemed to be filled with lumps and he could only swallow real hard and blow his nose loudly. But the others saw a sunny light of happiness shining through his eyes.

After all had kissed each other goodbye, the jumping boat jumped away and in a short time everything began getting darker and darker.

"We must be going to have a terrible rain storm," Raggedy Andy said.

"No, no," the Fairy Princess laughed. "That is not the reason it is getting darker and darker. You see, I am just sending the jumping boat back from today to yesterday night; which, when we get there, will be the same time that it was when you left."

Raggedy Andy rubbed his head thoughtfully, but could not quite make it out, so he remained silent. So did Raggedy Ann. When the flying boat came to rest in the back yard, Raggedy Ann and Raggedy Andy and Babette kissed the Fairy Princess and the twelve Pirate Girls good-bye and ran through the grass and climbed into the play-room window.

All the other dolls were sound asleep, so Raggedy Ann and Babette and Raggedy Andy were as still as mice as they climbed into their dollie beds. Then after they had been quiet for a long time Raggedy Ann sat up and ran her rag arm through her yarn hair, then whispering to Raggedy Andy to follow her, Raggedy Ann and Raggedy Andy carefully crawled out of bed, climbed upon the window-sill and jumped "BLUMP" to the ground. Raggedy Ann picked herself up, shook the wrinkles from her dress and ran to the play-house, followed by Raggedy Andy. They jumped upon the doll-beds and bounced up and down as they smiled up at the wooden ceiling.

From outside came the songs of the little creatures who live in the grasses and the flowers and above these sounds Raggedy Ann and Raggedy Andy heard the "Squeek! Squeek! Squeekity-squeek!" of Johnny Cricket's fiddle as Johnny bounced up and down upon his seat on a tall blade of grass. And Raggedy Ann and Raggedy Andy did not feel a bit lonesome out there all alone, for Raggedy Ann and Raggedy Andy were thinking lovely, kind, beautiful thoughts. And when one is thinking lovely, kind, beautiful thoughts of course one has no time to become lonesome.

THE END

RAGGEDY ANN'S WISHING PEBBLE

Written and Illustrated
by

JOHNNY GRUELLE

" " " " " " To Mary Katherine Fred Who Hears the Whispers of the Humming Bird Fairies, This Adventure is Affectionately Dedicated." " " " " "

INTRODUCTION TO WISHING PEBBLE

RAGGEDY ANN and Raggedy Andy were two little rag dolls. Very quiet little creatures; stuffed with nice white cotton. They had bright shoe button eyes and cheery, happy smiles painted upon their rag faces.

Raggedy Ann and Raggedy Andy were very happy little creatures, too, for they were over fifty years old and had always had so much fun in all their raggedy lives, they just couldn't help being joyous and kindly.

Raggedy Andy always said, "The reason Raggedy Ann is so lovable and kindly and generous and able to think so nicely, is because she has a candy heart with the words, 'I love you,' printed on it;" but Raggedy Andy was just as kindly and cheery and generous as dear Raggedy Ann and he has no candy heart.

And maybe it is just as Raggedy Ann has often said to the other dolls in the nursery, "If one just thinks nice, kindly things; if one just does generous, helpful deeds, then that person is filled with a thrill of happiness which shines right through even the shabbiest clothes and brings loving friends close by!"

* * * * *

One evening, all the dolls in the nursery, Raggedy Ann, Raggedy Andy, Henny, the Dutch doll, Fredarika, Uncle Clem (a very nice man doll with yarn moustache and a policeman's uniform) and the French doll and all the others, sat around telling stories.

And when it came to Raggedy Ann's turn, she told of the adventures she and Raggedy Andy had with the camel with the wrinkled knees. It was very exciting and so interesting none of the dolls closed their eyes even a smidgin while Raggedy Ann spoke in her soft, cottony, rag voice. Then, when Raggedy Ann had finished, she told all the dolls it was time they were in bed; and indeed, it was, for it was almost time for smiling Mister Sun to come peeping into the windows. So all the dolls hurried and jumped into bed, in just the same positions their little Mistress, Marcella, had placed them early in the evening. In a few minutes everything was so still you could have heard the patter of a teeny weeny mouse if he had "trip-tripped" across the floor. Then Raggedy Andy raised up on his cotton stuffed elbow and whispered to Raggedy Ann, "Less have another adventure! Shall we?"

And Raggedy Ann's shoe button eyes wiggled with pleasure and she whispered in reply, "Yes, Raggedy Andy! Less do!" So they tiptoed quietly to the window, climbed to the sill and catching hands jumped to the ground below,

"BLUMP! BLUMP!" And so this adventure began.

Let us start a garden, you and I.
Let us turn the soil of acquaintanceship
And in this fertile ground plant kindly thoughts;
Let us pull all weeds of envy and selfishness
And destroy them!
Let us water our garden with the dew of sympathy.
Let us keep our growing plants in the sunshine of love
And happiness is ours; our garden is filled
With the beautiful flowers of friendship

THE ADVENTURES OF RAGGEDY ANN AND RAGGEDY ANDY

RAGGEDY ANN and Raggedy Andy went skipping over the Yellow Meadow; each with a rag arm around the other's neck. When the two Raggedys reached a clump of Golden Rod they heard tiny voices, laughing and singing.

"Sh!" both Raggedys whispered to each other as they crept up closer.

"You need not be so quiet!" a teeny weeny silvery voice called to them from the Golden Rod, "We can see you easily, and knew you were coming!"

Raggedy Ann and Raggedy Andy laughed happily as they pushed aside the Golden Rod and saw hundreds of cunning little Brownies. "We did not know who it might be," said Raggedy Ann, "And we did not wish to frighten you away until we saw who you were."

"And then did you wish to frighten us away?" one of the tiny Brownies asked. Raggedy Ann and Raggedy Andy laughed as cheerily as all the Brownies at this. "No, indeed!" Raggedy Ann said when they had stopped laughing, "We did not wish to have you quit your happy games! That's what I meant to say, so we were just tiptoeing up easily, and then we would have gone away!"

"Well! We are glad you came!" one of the little Brownie men said, "for you can join in our fun!" "Thank you!" the two Raggedys cried, "We like fun! What were you playing?"

"We were just planning to fly down to the Looking Glass Brook and slide on the water, so you may go with us!"

"We would like to go," Raggedy Andy answered, "But we cannot fly, nor can we slide upon the surface of the water without getting wet; but then that's fun too, because our rag bodies are stuffed with nice white cotton and we soon dry out in the lovely warm sunshine!"

The little Brownies laughed and one said, "When you slide with us, you won't get even a little teeny weeny speck wet!" And waving his hand to the other Brownies, he caught Raggedy Andy's hand; other little Brownies caught Raggedy Andy's feet and Raggedy Ann's hands and feet and whisked them up over the Golden Rod and out across the Yellow Meadow to the Looking Glass Brook.

When the little Brownies and the two Raggedys reached the Looking Glass Brook, they all ran as hard as they could and went sliding across the smooth surface of the water. It was just like sliding upon ice, except when one of the Brownies or one of the Raggedys fell down, they bounced up again; for the surface of the Looking Glass Brook gave beneath them like rubber ice and they did not get their heads bumped. As they slid along upon the top of the water, Raggedy Ann and Raggedy Andy could see the pretty little fish swimming about and chasing each other back and forth just as if they were having games too.

The Raggedys and the little Brownies were not the only ones who were sliding upon the surface of the water, for while they were resting, they saw queer little tiny long-legged creatures come sliding along. And one came right up to the Brownies and Raggedy Ann and Andy. "Why! He has a tiny boat on each of his feet!" Andy cried in surprise.

"Oh, yes!" a little Brownie said, "He's one of the little Ferry-men!"

"Do you mean that he carries tiny passengers across the Looking Glass Brook?" asked Raggedy Ann. "That is just what they do!" laughed the little Brownies. "You see, many little creatures cannot walk upon the water, and, if they happen to fall into the water and try to swim across, the little fish, sometimes-most-always eat them up!"

"So the little Ferry-men, or 'Water Boatmen,' as they are sometimes called, run from one point upon the Looking Glass Brook to another point and they carry passengers, for the fish never disturb the Ferry-men!"

"And I suppose the tiny creatures pay the little Ferry-men with seeds or something like that!" said Raggedy Andy.

"Oh no!" laughed the little Brownies, "The little Ferry-men never ask pay for carrying the tiny creatures across, because you see, they get so much fun out of sliding across the Looking Glass Brook themselves so that is all the pay they wish." When the little Brownies told the Raggedys that it was time they went to work, each little Brownie gave the rag dolls a kiss. Each kiss left a tiny brown freckle on each of the Raggedys' faces, just like the little faces of boys and girls who have been kissed by the Brownies. Then with a lot of tiny Brownie whoops, the cunning creatures flew high in the air and across the meadow, leaving the two Raggedys watching the little kindly Water Boatmen carrying the tiny bug passengers across the Looking Glass Brook.

And the Raggedys, with an arm about each other's neck felt that their little cotton stuffed heads were filled with happiness, for you know how much pleasure it gives YOU when you see someone doing unselfish deeds and kindly acts for those in need. And even if it is only a very, very tiny little deed of kindness, the Raggedys knew that however small they may be, the kindly deeds grow and grow until they blossom and fill our hearts with the sunshine of Happiness.

JOHNNY
GRUELLE

CHAPTER TWO

AS THE Raggedys sat upon the bank of the Looking Glass Brook and watched the little Water Boatmen carry the tiny creatures across, a ripple came circling by them, then another and another until the little Water Boatmen rocked as they slid over the tops of the ripples. "It looks just as if the Looking Glass Brook was smiling!" laughed Raggedy Ann.

Then as the ripples came faster and faster and closer together, the two Raggedys peeked over the edge of the bending grasses and saw a queer little dumpy creature standing in the water and digging a hole in the bank. He wore a little round felt hat and worked in his shirt sleeves. The Raggedys could not see the little dumpy creature's face until they spoke to him and he looked up at them. Then they saw it was Mister Muskrat and his bright little eyes danced laughingly behind round spectacles. "What ever are you doing, Mister Muskrat?" Raggedy Ann asked, "You are making the Looking Glass Brook dance and ripple just as if it was giggling!"

Mister Muskrat pulled his suspenders over his shoulders and winked slowly at both rag dolls. "Who knows?" he smiled, "Perhaps it is giggling at me, for you know, someone just played a prank on me!"

"But I believe I know who it was!" Mister Muskrat went on, as he pushed his little round hat back and wiped his forehead with his red pocket hanky.

"Who do you s'pect?" asked Raggedy Andy.

"Well," laughed Mister Muskrat, "When I came here to my kitchen door a few minutes ago, I found that someone had filled my doorway with pieces of mud and grass and completely closed it as tight as tight could be, and in the soft dirt all around the doorway, I saw the tracks where whoever did it had walked, and I said, 'ha ha, I know who made those foot prints! It was Timothy Turtle'."

"How did you know that it was Timothy?" Raggedy

Ann wished to know. "Cause you see," said Mister Muskrat, "Timothy Turtle wears four shoes, two on his front feet and two on his back feet and he turns them in pigeon toed when he walks. So you see, he left four pigeon-toed tracks! And now I'm digging my kitchen doorway open again, for it is time I had my dinner!" "What will you do with Timothy Turtle when you catch him, Mister Muskrat?" Raggedy Andy asked. Mister Muskrat stuck his spade in the bank and sat down beside the two Raggedys. "Timothy Turtle is a funny fellow!" Mister Muskrat chuckled. "He plays a prank on someone and then he walks away a few feet and pulls his head into his collar, so that just his nose peeks out and because he keeps his eyes closed, Timothy believes that no one can see him! Then he usually goes to sleep and forgets all about what he has done. If you will peep just around the bend in the bank, you will see Timothy Turtle sound asleep and right where I had to pass him when I came to my kitchen doorway!" "And didn't you even awaken him?" Andy asked.

"Oh no!" laughed Mister Muskrat, "You know that Timothy Turtle carries his house right upon his back all the time, and he gets very tired, so he needs all the sleep he can get!"

Just then Timothy Turtle came walking pigeon-toed around the bend in the bank and tipped his hat to Raggedy

Ann, although to do this he had to take off one of his shoes. Timothy Turtle sounded like a polly parrot when he talked and although the Raggedys had to smile (for their smiles were painted on) they were careful not to laugh at Timothy's funny voice. "Well, here you are hard at work, Mister Muskrat! Building a new house I suppose?"

Mister Muskrat winked at the Raggedys and said, "Sit down here beside our two friends, Timothy Turtle, and I will soon be through!" And with this Mister Muskrat made the dirt fly until he had opened his kitchen doorway. Then he went inside and came out with two large slices of Muskrat bread and butter and jam and gave one to Timothy Turtle.

"I know that you two Raggedys do not eat!" he laughed, "And if I give you a bite, it would get jam all over your painted faces!" "Thank you just the same!" Raggedy Ann and Andy both replied.

When Timothy Turtle had eaten his slice of bread, he said, "Guess I'll swim out to the log and take a nap in the nice warm sunshine!" and nodding his head gravely to the two rag dolls and Mister Muskrat, Timothy Turtle walked pigeon-toed down the bank, into the water and swam lazily out to the log. "You see!" laughed Mister Muskrat, "Timothy Turtle had forgotten all about playing his prank on me!"

"I think the nicest part is that you forgive him for making you so much unnecessary work!" Raggedy Ann laughed.

"Oh, really there was nothing for me to forgive!" Mister Muskrat replied, "For I have all the time I wish and I love to work, so if Timothy Turtle got some fun out of it, then I don't mind in the least, for I have the fun of undoing what he did. And don't you see, if I should get angry at Timothy, that would have taken all the pleasure out of my work, for then I might not have wanted to work. And when anyone tries to get out of a little bit of work which he has to do, or when he puts it off until some other time, then it seems as though the work which is put off, grows and grows until it takes ever so much longer to do."

CHAPTER THREE

"MAY we come into your house and see how you live?" Raggedy Andy asked of Mister Muskrat. "Why, Andy!" Raggedy Ann laughed, "Don't you know that is very impolite?" Raggedy Andy fidgeted his foot about in the sand and did not know just what to say, but Mister Muskrat patted him upon the back and laughed, "That's all right, Raggedy Andy, I was just about to ask both of you inside for it looks to me as if we were about to have a heavy rain, and if you stay out in the rain, I am sure your rag bodies will get very soggy!" And with this Mister Muskrat led the way into his kitchen.

"Isn't it nice and cozy in here?" Raggedy Ann exclaimed. "It is so quiet you can hardly hear any of the sounds from the creatures along the Looking Glass Brook!" "That's one reason why I like it!" Mister Muskrat answered, leading the way up a long hall into a larger room. "This is my living room!" And he pulled out two little chairs for the Raggedys and took an easy chair himself. After lighting his Muskrat pipe, the funny, dumpy creature crossed his feet and leaned back comfortably. "Yes, indeedy! Timothy Turtle is a queer little fellow, and all his turtle relatives are queer little creatures, too But then," continued Mister Muskrat, "probably Timothy Turtle and his relatives think everyone else is queer, too. And I guess it is just as well that we do think that way, for if we didn't we'd probably be discontented and want to be changed into something else. And, that is just how the Turtle family happen to be as queer as they are. For, once upon a time, the Turtles were almost like the Hoppytoads and the Greenfrogs except that the Turtles could not hop as far as the Frogs. Then when larger creatures came to the streams where the Turtles and Hoppytoads and Frogs lived, the Turtles could not get into the water as fast as the Greenfrogs.

"And so, when Old Mister Skooligan, the Magician, came along one day, the Turtle family all cried, 'Oh, Mister

Skooligan, the mosquitoes bite us upon our backs and we can't hop fast enough to get away from them, and when Old Mister Heron comes along looking for dinner, we can't hop fast enough to get away from him! Can you give us some magic medicine which will make our backs so hard the mosquitoes can't bite us and Old Mister Heron won't be able to eat us for dinner?' And Old Mister Skooligan, the Magician, he winked his eyes behind his glasses and he chuckled to himself. 'Humm! Less see!' musin' like and then he took out his magic pocket book with two magic suspender buttons and three glass beads in it and touched each Turtle upon the back. 'There!' he said, 'Now the mosquitoes can't bite you, and Mister Heron won't care to eat you!' And away he walked. And so", continued Mister Muskrat as he puffed the smoke up around the ceiling, "the Turtle family got just what they asked for but not exactly what they wanted, and while they have very hard backs, they get very tired carrying such heavy loads about with them all the time!"

"They should have been satisfied!" said Raggedy Andy, "then probably Old Mister Skooligan would have changed them to something even better without them asking for a change!"

"And that's why all the Turtle family are so slow and

sleepy!" mused Raggedy Ann, "I've wondered how they became that way!"

"But there's one thing about the Turtles!" said Mister Muskrat, "if they start out to do anything, they keep plodding away until it is done!"

"Do the Turtles have any homes besides the ones they carry upon their backs?" asked Raggedy Andy.

"No!" laughed Mister Muskrat, "Unless the mud they bury themselves in at the bottom of the streams in the winter time could be called homes!"

"Then, too," he added, "A lot of the Turtles come into our homes for the winter and pull their heads and feet into their shells and sleep!"

"It is kind of you to let them stay with you all winter, Mister Muskrat," Raggedy Ann said.

"Well," Mister Muskrat replied, "The Turtles come in very handy to us at times during the winter!"

Raggedy Ann and Raggedy Andy laughed at this and asked "How?"

"Lots and lots of times we Muskrats have parties and then we use the sleeping turtles for seats and they never know it at all!"

Just then Missus Muskrat came walking in with a basket upon her arm, "My! It's raining hard outside!" she said after shaking hands with the two rag dolls, "You Raggedys had better stay all night with us!"

"Thank you, Missus Muskrat!" Raggedy Ann and Andy replied, "We will if it will not put you to any bother!"

"Dear me, no!" laughed the two Muskrats, "We have plenty of spare bed rooms!" And they took the two rag dolls and tucked them in little beds as comfortable as could be and wishing them goodnight, Mister and Missus Muskrat tiptoed out, leaving the two Raggedys, their little rag heads filled with kindly thoughts and their shoe-button eyes staring up at the ceiling.

"Isn't it nice to meet people who are so unselfish!" Raggedy Andy whispered to Raggedy Ann. "Indeed it is!" Raggedy Ann answered, "It makes my little candy heart feel like it would bump right through my pretty white apron. And if we are kind and unselfish, then those who meet us will be filled with good thoughts and love for us!"

"I met Gerty Gartersnake yesterday!" said Missus Muskrat at the breakfast table as she passed the pancakes to Raggedy Ann, "And she had a lovely new dress!" "I didn't know Gerty Gartersnake ever had new clothes!" laughed Raggedy Ann as she poured maple syrup upon the pancake.

"Oh yes!" Missus Muskrat replied, "Every once in a while she gets new clothes!" "But she has no hands to make them with!" Raggedy Andy said. "Does some kind creature make them for her?"

Mister and Missus Muskrat chuckled at this, "Yes, indeed, my dears!" said Missus Muskrat, "The kindest person in the world makes them for her, 'Mother Nature!' "

"Isn't that nice!" Raggedy Ann cried, "Mother Nature must be very kind."

"Indeed she is!" agreed Missus Muskrat. "If it wasn't for Mother Nature some of the poor creatures would have a very hard time! As it is, Gertrude Gartersnake has a hard time getting off her old clothes, for you see her new clothes are always under her old clothes!"

"How strange!" said Raggedy Ann, "You would think the new clothes would be on the outside, like children's dresses, and then you would take off the old dress and put on the new!"

"That is probably the way children have to get their new clothes!" Missus Muskrat nodded her funny head, "But Mother Nature plans it better for her tiny creatures. She makes the new clothes upon Gerty Gartersnake right in under her old clothes, so all Gerty has to do, is take off her old dress and she has her new one on without the bother of putting it on!"

"I always thought that Gerty Gartersnake wore her dresses much too tight!" Mister Muskrat said with a sly wink at Raggedy Andy.

Missus Muskrat knew that Mister Muskrat was joking, so she gave Mister Muskrat a pancake with a hole in it and said, "Gerty Gartersnake does not even have to button her new dress, it fits her without buttons. But, My! How Gerty Gartersnake has to wiggle and twist to get out of her old dress!"

"Lots of times, children find Gerty's old dresses lying around and I suppose they wonder how Gerty ever gets out of them."

"There's someone tapping at the kitchen door!" said Mister Muskrat as he got up from the table and went to the door. "Well, if it isn't Gerty Gartersnake herself, with her pretty new dress on!"

"We were just speaking of you!" said Raggedy Ann as she pulled up a chair for Gerty Gartersnake to sit upon. "Mister Muskrat says he thinks your clothes fit you too tight!" said Raggedy Andy.

"If Mister Muskrat wasn't so nice, I'd think he was teasing me!" said Gerty Gartersnake, as she tasted the pancakes and maple syrup, "But he knows very well that if I did not wear real tight clothes, Why!—I'd be catching them on every twig and stick that I wiggled over! Yes, indeed, my clothes are very smooth and tight, but that is just the way I need them so that I can wiggle along and not get fastened upon anything and everything!"

"Your dress is very pretty!" said Raggedy Ann.

"I think it is too!" Gerty Gartersnake laughed, "Mother Nature in the far-off beginning took different flowers and made the first Gartersnake dress and that is why our dresses are covered with such pretty red and yellow colors! We can hide right in amongst the pretty flowers and it is very hard for anyone to see us."

"You don't bite people, do you, Gerty Gartersnake?"

Raggedy Andy asked.

Gerty Gartersnake almost wiggled off the Muskrat's chair she laughed so hard. "Dear me, no! I don't bite anything except things I wish to eat, like pancakes."

When everyone had eaten as many pancakes and maple syrup as they wished Missus Muskrat and Raggedy Ann washed and wiped the dishes while Gerty Gartersnake wrapped a rag around her tail and dusted the furniture.

Mister Muskrat and Raggedy Andy swept the floors all nice and clean and put the dishes in the Muskrat cupboard. Then when everything was nice and tidy, they all went out upon the Muskrat's back porch and watched the pretty fish jumping about in the Looking Glass Brook.

"How nice it is just to sit here and listen to all the music of Nature!" said Raggedy Andy.

"Yes, indeed!" Raggedy Ann agreed, "It's just like a great, great, big music box which old Mister Sun winds up every evening before he goes to bed, so that it will start bright and early in the morning playing and sending out happy sounds for everyone's pleasure."

CHAPTER FOUR

RAGGEDY Ann and Raggedy Andy thanked Missus and Mister Muskrat for the nice time they had at the Muskrat home and after shaking hands good bye, the two rag dolls walked along the edge of the Looking Glass Brook. They peeped under the overhanging grasses and poked about in the sand and pebbles along the shore. "I wish that we could find a wishing pebble!" said Raggedy Andy.

"Dear me! What would two rag dolls do with a Wishing Pebble?" Raggedy Ann wanted to know.

"Why!" laughed Raggedy Andy, "We could wish for so many nice pretty things like Lolly-pops and ice cream cones and soda water and candy and toys and everything like that!"

"Then let's hunt for a Wishing Pebble!" said Raggedy Ann, "Do you know what they look like, Raggedy Andy?"

"Of course I have never seen one!" Raggedy Andy replied, "But I have heard that they are round and smooth and real white.

"Is this one, do you suppose, Raggedy Andy?" Raggedy Ann asked as she held up a white pebble.

"Less see!" Raggedy Andy said as he held out his rag hand for the pebble. "Well, it's nice and white, Raggedy Ann and it's quite smooth, but it isn't round enough I'm 'fraid!"

"I'll keep it anyway," Raggedy Ann laughed as she put the pretty pebble in her apron pocket, "For it may be a Wishing Pebble and we would not know it!"

"We can easily find out if it is a Wishing Pebble!" said Raggedy Andy.

"How?" asked Raggedy Ann as she took the pretty pebble from her pocket.

"Why!" said Raggedy Andy, "When you find a Wishing Pebble, you must hold it tight in your hand and close your eyes tightly and make a wish. Then if it is a real for sure, truly Wishing Pebble, whatever you wish for comes true!"

"Then", said Raggedy Ann, "Let's wish for something and see if it comes true!"

"All right!" Raggedy Andy agreed, "You wish for something!"

"But I don't know what to wish for!" Raggedy Ann laughed, "There's nothing I need!"

"Then wish for something for Missus Muskrat!" Raggedy Andy suggested. "Why not wish for her to have a magic pancake mixer which will always be full of pancakes ready to cook!"

"All right!" agreed Raggedy Ann, "I'll wish that Missus Muskrat had a very magical pancake mixer always filled with pancakes ready to be cooked!"

"Oh, wait a minute!" Raggedy Andy cried, "I thought of something better! Wish that the pancakes were already cooked, then Missus Muskrat won't have to even bother about cooking them!"

"But s'pose she really likes to do her own pancake making!" said Raggedy Ann, "Then if we give her a magic pancake mixer filled with pancakes all ready cooked, she wouldn't have the fun making them any more!"

"I hadn't thought of that, Raggedy Ann!" Andy said, "Less see!"

"Anyway!" Raggedy Ann shook her head, "We can't make the Wishing Pebble work!" "Why?" asked Raggedy Andy.

"Cause! We can't close our shoe-button eyes when we make a wish!" said Raggedy Ann. "HMMMM!" was all Andy could say, but he sat down in the sand and ran his rag hand up through his yarn hair and tried to think of a way.

"I can't think of any way at all!" laughed Raggedy Ann, "Shoe-button eyes can't close, and that's all there is to it!"

Raggedy Andy finally hopped up in the air and turned a flip-flop; it wasn't a very good flip-flop, for Raggedy Andy only turned partly over in the air and fell with his rag legs twisted over his head. When Raggedy Ann had straightened him out, he laughed and said, "We can have the fun of wishing anyway, Raggedy Ann, and if we wish for things, nice things for others, we can pretend the wishes come true!"

"That is a nice thought!" Raggedy Ann laughed, "So I wish Gerty Gartersnake had a new dress!" "And I wish all the birds would sing!" said Raggedy Andy.

"And I wish the Muskrats had a magic soda-water fountain in their living room!" said Raggedy Ann.

"And I wish they had a lolly-pop field right out back of their kitchen door!" said Raggedy Andy. "And now, Raggedy Ann, let's run back to the Muskrats' house and see if our wishes came true!"

"No! Less not!" Raggedy Ann said in her soft Raggedy voice, "It's much more fun in not knowing, for don't you see, if we don't know for sure, we can still believe our wishes have come true and we have the pleasure of having wished for good things for our friends!"

JOHNNY GRUELLE

CHAPTER FIVE

"WHAT do you think?" asked Freddy Fieldmouse as he ran up to where the two Raggedys sat upon the clean sand at the edge of the Looking-Glass Brook.

"We were thinking a lot of happy thoughts, Freddy Fieldmouse!" Raggedy Ann laughingly replied.

Freddy Fieldmouse laughed too as he said, "That is very, very nice, I'm sure, Raggedys, but I mean what do you think about Mister and Missus Muskrat?"

"We think they are nice and very kindly!" said Raggedy Andy.

"Yes! I know they are very nice and unselfish, Raggedys, but I mean—what do you think the Muskrats have?"

"Hmmm!" mused Raggedy Ann, "Is this a riddle, or something like that, Freddy Fieldmouse?"

"No-siree-bob!" cried Freddy Fieldmouse, "You wouldn't guess in a long, long time!"

"Is it a new Muskrat baby?" asked Raggedy Ann.

"Nope!" Freddy Fieldmouse replied.

"Then we give up!" said Raggedy Andy, "I felt a stitch rip out of my rag head, I guessed so hard!"

Raggedy Ann carefully looked at Raggedy Andy's head,

even taking off his little blue and white cap to see better, "You haven't lost a single stitch, Raggedy Andy!" she laughed, "You mustn't try to fool us that way!"

"Well!" laughed Raggedy Andy, "I give up anyway, I can't guess what the Muskrats have!"

"I won't give up!" said Raggedy Ann, "But please tell us anyway, Freddy Fieldmouse."

"Then I guess I'll tell you!" agreed Freddy Fieldmouse, "But I 'spect you'll be s'prised! When I was swinging upon a swingy weed right over the Muskrat's kitchen door, I heard Missus Muskrat squeal and I almost fell off the weed into the water thinking that something had her!"

"What was it, Freddy Fieldmouse?" Raggedy Andy asked.

"I was just about to tell you," Freddy Fieldmouse replied.

"Just you be patient, Raggedy Andy!" Raggedy Ann said jokingly, as she pushed Andy's little blue and white cap down over his shoe-button eyes.

"I am!" Raggedy Andy laughed, "But I am so anxious to know why Missus Muskrat squealed as if something had her!"

"I climbed back up the swinging weed and ran down towards the Muskrat's kitchen door and peeped through the grass, but Missus Muskrat had run in the house and Mister Muskrat had run in after her. I could hear them both squealing and I said to myself, 'the Muskrats are squeal ing because they are happy. That's what!' and I walked right in without knocking and what do you think!"

"Dear me, Freddy Fieldmouse! If you don't tell us what you think instead of asking us what WE think, I'm sure to rip all the stitches out of my rag head trying to guess!" said Raggedy Andy.

"When I walked into the Muskrats' house and into their living room, there stood Missus Muskrat with one in her hand and Mister Muskrat with one in his hand and when they saw me, they put one in my hand—"

"Not three Muskrat babies?" Raggedy Ann said.

"No-siree-bob! Three ice cream sodas, that's what!" said Freddy Fieldmouse.

Raggedy Andy jumped up and danced about in the sand, kicking his rag feet so high in the air, he almost fell in the Looking-Glass Brook and Raggedy Ann just sat still and smiled. "Wasn't that enough to make anyone squeal, to find an ice cream soda fountain right in their living room?" asked Freddy Fieldmouse. "We are very, very glad!" said Raggedy Ann, "And how do you s'pose the soda-water fountain ever happened to be in the Muskrat's living room, Freddy Fieldmouse?"

"Missus Muskrat told me that she was sitting in the arm-chair darning Mister Muskrat's socks when she heard a funny sizzling noise right in back of her, and she jumped up so quick she upset her darning basket and ran out to the kitchen porch. Then she said to Mister Muskrat, 'There's a sizzler in our living room!' And Mister Muskrat picked up a stick so that he might have something to poke the sizzler with, if it needed polking, but when they both got in their living room again, they soon saw that the sizzling noise came from the pretty little soda-water fountain, and we drank sodas until we had enough!"

"You still have some soda-water, or ice cream on your chin!" said Raggedy Ann, and she dipped her hand into the Looking-Glass Brook and washed Freddy Fieldmouse's face.

"I'm running to tell everybody and invite them to the Muskrat's house to eat ice cream sodas!" said Freddy Fieldmouse as he jumped through the grass.

"Well what do you think?" asked Raggedy Andy.

"I am thinking a lot of happy thoughts!" Raggedy Ann laughingly replied.

"Yes, I am too!" said Raggedy Andy, "But don't you think our Wishing Pebble must have been a real, for-sure Wishing Pebble after all? You know we wished that the Muskrats would have an ice cream soda water fountain in their living room!"

"Then I guess it must have been a Wishing Pebble!" said Raggedy Ann, "And I wish that I had kept it now! I thought it was only a make believe Wishing Pebble and I buried it in the sand again!"

"Well we have had that much fun with it anyway!" laughed Raggedy Andy, "And we should be happy of that. Indeed whenever we give pleasure to others, we always make happiness for ourselves!"

And the two Raggedys' shoe-button eyes twinkled merrily.

CHAPTER SIX

"LESS run down to Mister and Missus Muskrat's home and see their new ice cream soda water fountain!" said Raggedy Andy as he lifted Raggedy Ann to her feet.

"You are just in time, Raggedy Ann and Raggedy Andy!" cried Missus Muskrat, "We have had sixteen ice cream sodas already and Mister Muskrat is going to have one more!"

"I've had every flavor except pineapple!" laughed Mister Muskrat, "and I want to try that! Then I will rest up for about fifteen minutes and try them all over again!"

"I wish you rag dolls could eat ice cream!" said Missus Muskrat, "You can't imagine how good it tastes!"

"I wish that we could," Raggedy Ann sighed, "But you know we haven't any real, for-sure mouths like you folks and when we taste anything, it just runs and soaks in our rag faces."

"Then we have to be scrubbed!" laughed Raggedy Andy.

"Don't you think if we made a little teeny-weeny hole in the center of your mouths, we could put a straw in the hole and you could taste the sodas?" Mister Muskrat asked.

"We might try it!" Raggedy Ann agreed.

"I can sew the hole up again after you have tasted the sodas if you wish!" said Missus Muskrat.

Mister Muskrat set down his glass of soda-water and ran to his tool-box and brought back a large nail. "Now I can poke this nail right in the center of your mouths and make a hole large enough to put a straw in!"

"Won't it hurt them?" Missus Muskrat asked.

"Not even a tiny speck!" Raggedy Andy laughed, "Our heads are nothing but cloth stuffed with nice white, clean cotton! And besides, we often get rips in our heads and bodies! No indeed, Missus Muskrat, It won't hurt at all!" So Mister Muskrat soon poked two holes in the Raggedys' mouths with his nail and Missus Muskrat filled two glasses with vanilla soda. "For" she explained, "If the vanilla soaks through the cotton, it won't stain as much as strawberry, or raspberry or chocolate!"

It was easy for Raggedy Ann and Raggedy Andy to drink the lovely ice cream soda through a straw and they were surprised after drinking two glasses apiece to find that the soda did not soak through to the back of their rag heads.

"Dear Me!" Raggedy Ann exclaimed as she held out her glass for more, "Just think of what we have missed all these years, Raggedy Andy!"

"That is just what I have been thinking!" laughed Raggedy Andy, "And I was also thinking that I would like to try a glass of raspberry soda!"

"I don't believe it will soak through any more than the vanilla did!" Raggedy Ann replied, "So I guess that I will have a strawberry soda!"

"While you folks sit here and have all the sodas you wish!" said Mister Muskrat, "I'll just run around the neighborhood and ask everybody in to have sodas!"

Raggedy Ann and Raggedy Andy had hardly finished their ninth glass of soda-water when the neighbors began trooping into the Muskrat home, so then the Raggedys had to quit in order to help Missus and Mister Muskrat serve the neighbors with the different flavors.

"I tell you what, Raggedy Ann and Raggedy Andy," cried Mister Muskrat, "I don't know how this magic soda-water fountain came in our living room, but I'm very happy and thankful that it is here, for now all our friends can come in any time and help themselves to all the sodas they wish!"

"Raggedy Ann wished the soda-water fountain in here for you!" Raggedy Andy told Mister and Missus Muskrat.

"Do your wishes come true?" all the neighbors of the Muskrats wished to know.

"I wish that they did!" laughed Raggedy Ann, "For there are a lot of wishes I would like to make!"

"Raggedy Ann found a Wishing Pebble!" said Raggedy Andy, "And she wished for a few things!" Of course everybody wanted to see the wonderful wishing pebble and they were so disappointed when Raggedy Ann told them that she had buried the wonderful pebble in the sand.

"I do not believe I would ever be able to find it again!" she laughed.

"We'll all go and help you find it!" said Mister Muskrat, "Just as soon as we all have six more glasses apiece!"

"The nice part about the Magic Soda-water Fountain," said Missus Muskrat, "Is that you can drink about fifteen glasses and it never makes your stomach ache!"

"I think the nicest part of it is that all your friends have been asked to share in your pleasures!" laughed Raggedy Ann.

And all the friends of Mister and Missus Muskrat agreed to this, for every one knows how nice it is to have free ice-cream sodas whenever they wish them, and especially magic ice cream sodas that never give anyone the stomach ache.

CHAPTER SEVEN

"WHEE!" Raggedy Ann cried, after she and Andy had drank fifteen glasses of soda-water from Mister Muskrat's magic soda-water fountain," I don't believe I can drink another soda!"

"They were so good!" Raggedy Andy laughed, "But I guess that I have had enough for now!"

Mister and Missus Muskrat and all their neighbors said that they had all the sodas they wished for. "Let's go out and see if we can find the Wishing Pebble where Raggedy Ann buried it in the sand!" suggested Mister Muskrat; "Then when we find it, we will all be thirsty again and we can all come back in here and have more sodas!"

"That's a fine idea!" cried Missus Muskrat, "And if we find the Wishing Pebble we can wish for everything! Let's hurry and find it!" So out the door she ran, followed by Raggedy Ann and Raggedy Andy and Mister Muskrat and all their neighbors. There was Georgie Groundhog and Henrietta Hedgehog and Charlie Chipmunk and Freddie Field-mouse and Freda Field-mouse and all the rest of the neighbors. They ran out the door in a long string and raced down the bank toward the sandy shore where Raggedy Ann and Raggedy Andy had found the Wishing Pebble.

"Here's where we were sitting when we found the pebble!" said Raggedy Ann, "But I can't remember where I was when we made the wishes, or where I was when I buried the Wishing Pebble in the sand!"

"Then we must hunt all along the sandy stretch of shore!" said Georgie Groundhog as he began scratching the sand right and left.

"I guess we had better all hunt a little distance apart from each other!" laughed Henrietta Hedgehog, as she brushed the sand from her dress where Georgie Groundhog had kicked it.

"We can find it easier if we search farther apart!" said Missus Muskrat. "I'll scratch up the sand over here!" And soon all the friends were sending the sand in all directions as they dug for the magic wishing pebble.

Raggedy Ann looked over to where Georgie Groundhog had been digging and all she could see of him was his tail sticking out of a hole in the sand and he was sending the sand up from the bottom of the hole in a shower.

"Oh say, Georgie Groundhog!" Raggedy Ann laughed, "Stop digging for a minute!"

"Have you found it, Raggedy Ann?" Georgie Groundhog wished to know as he climbed out of the hole he had dug, his face all covered with wet sand.

"No we haven't found it, Georgie!" Raggedy Ann laughed as she brushed the sand from his face with her apron. And as the others all came and listened Raggedy Ann said, "When I buried the magic Wishing Pebble I just pushed it down under the loose sand, so when we find it, it will only be about an inch under the surface."

"And here I was scratching and digging a regular tunnel!" laughed Georgie Groundhog.

"We must just feel around in the loose sand!" said Raggedy Andy, "And when we find it, it probably will be right near the top!"

"Yes, it will!" said Raggedy Ann, "I remember that I had just wished that a garden of lolly-pops would be growing right at Missus Muskrat's kitchen door and then I pushed it right under the sand, for I thought it wasn't a real for sure Wishing Pebble!"

"Isn't it too bad, you didn't know?" Henrietta Hedgehog said.

"But there were no Lolly-pops growing at our kitchen door!" said Mister Muskrat, "For I came in and went out of the kitchen door many times and if the Lolly-pops had been growing there I know I would have seen them!"

"Surely they must be there!" said Henrietta Hedgehog, "Cause if Raggedy Ann wished for the magic Soda-water Fountain and it came in your house, surely the Lolly-pops must have come too!"

"I'll run and see!" said Mister Muskrat.

"Let's all run and see!" cried Missus Muskrat.

"I knew there were no Lolly-pops growing here!" said Mister Muskrat as he and his friends came to the Muskrat's kitchen door.

Raggedy Ann ran her rag hand up through her yarn hair and thought and thought, "I can't understand," she said, "Why one wish came true and not the other!" "Let's all go in the living room and have another glass of ice cream soda!" said Missus Muskrat, "Then perhaps we can think better!"

"Yes, let's do," cried Georgie Groundhog, "We can think a whole lot better if we have a soda!"

"Oh dear me, suzz!" Missus Muskrat cried when she walked into the living room, "There is'nt any Magic Soda-water Fountain any more!"

"It's gone!" cried all the neighbors.

"Ha! Ha! Ha!" a voice sounded in through the kitchen door, "Of course it's gone!"

"Who was that?" Raggedy Andy shouted.

"There is no one around here that I can see!" said Henrietta Hedgehog as she and the others came out of the Muskrat's house.

"Ha! Ha! Ha!" the voice again laughed from across the Looking Glass Brook, "I saw Raggedy Ann find the Magic Wishing Pebble and when she buried it, I soon found it! And I wished the Lolly-pops would disappear and the Magic Soda-water Fountain, too. And I've got the Wishing Pebble!"

"Don't cry!" Raggedy Ann said to Missus Muskrat, "We will find who it is and get the Pebble back!"

CHAPTER EIGHT

MISSUS MUSKRAT couldn't keep from crying, "I had planned on all of our friends coming in whenever they wished and helping themselves to the magic soda-water!" she sobbed.

"It is so nice to have a cold glass of ice cream soda on a hot day!" said Mister Muskrat, as he wiped his eyes with his red bandanna hankie.

"Well! Let's be thankful that we had a nice lot of ice cream sodas anyhow!" said Henrietta Hedgehog.

"I wonder who the disagreeable person is!" Raggedy Andy mused.

"I can't imagine!" Raggedy Ann replied, "I don't see why he didn't let the Muskrats have the Lolly-pop garden and the Ice Cream Soda-water Fountain; he could easily have wished for another just like it!"

"Whoever it is!" said Georgie Groundhog, "He must be very, very selfish and wants everything for himself and doesn't want anyone else to have any pleasures."

"I can't imagine who would be that selfish along the Looking Glass Brook!" said Missus Muskrat.

"I think it will be a good plan for all of us to try and find out who took the Magic Wishing Pebble, so that we can get it back!" said Raggedy Andy.

"If I find him, I shall throw him down and take it away from him!" said Georgie Groundhog.

"We mustn't do that!" said Raggedy Ann, "For you know, the Magic Wishing Pebble really belongs to whoever finds it! And while I had it, it belonged to me and when I buried it again, then, don't you see, it belonged to whoever found it the next time! So we must not take it away from him, for that would be wrong, even if he has wished the Magic Soda-water Fountain out of the Muskrat's living room!"

"Then how can we ever get it again?" Raggedy Andy wanted to know.

"First!" said Raggedy Ann, "We must find out who has it, then if he loses the Wishing Pebble, or if he buries it, as I did, if we can find it, it will belong to us and we can sit down and wish for a lot of things!"

"If I find it, I'm going to wish for a bicycle!" said Georgie Groundhog, "Then I can ride real fast up and down the paths through the yellow meadow.

"And I will wish for a pair of roller-skates!" said Henrietta Hedgehog, "Then Georgie and I can have lots of fun together!"

"I'll wish for the Soda-water Fountain back again!" said Missus Muskrat, "So that all our friends can have parties at our house!"

"I don't know what I shall wish for!" said Raggedy Ann thoughtfully, "But I'll probably think of something whenever I find the Magic Wishing Pebble!"

"I think we had all better hunt for the selfish person who has the Wishing Pebble!" said Raggedy Andy, "We can never find it by sitting here!"

"I'll start right out and find it!" said Georgie Groundhog, as he jumped to his feet, "And when I find it, I'll come right back here and let every one of you wish for as many things as you want!"

"Oh dear!" Missus Muskrat cried.

"Mercy me!" Henrietta Hedgehog squealed, for Georgie Groundhog had no more than got the words out of his mouth when his feet flew up in the air and he stood upon his head with his legs and arms waving about in a strange manner. Raggedy Ann and Raggedy Andy ran to Georgie Groundhog and pulled his feet down to the floor, but as soon as they let go of his feet, they flew up in the air again, so when they pulled Georgie's feet to the floor again Mister Muskrat sat upon them and held them there. "Whatever happened to you, Georgie?" he asked.

"I just flew upside down!" said Georgie, "And I tell you, it surely s'prised me!"

"How do you feel now?" asked Raggedy Ann.

"All right!" Georgie laughed.

Mister Muskrat got off of Georgie Groundhog's feet and Georgie stood up, but again his feet flew up in the air and he kicked his feet about trying to get them down to the floor. "It makes me dizzy!" he cried.

Raggedy Ann had been thinking as hard as her rag head could think, "Wait!" she said, "Cross your fingers, Georgie Groundhog!" she cried, "There! You see!" she laughed as Georgie Groundhog's feet came down to the floor and he was able to stand up again, "Whoever has the Magic Wishing Pebble knows that we want to get it back again and they are wishing for Georgie to stand upon his head! And, you know," whispered Raggedy Ann, "If you cross your fingers that means 'KING'S EX,' and you can't be Magicked at all!"

"Then!" said Raggedy Andy, "What will happen when one of US gets Magicked, Raggedy Ann?"

"I don't know!" laughed Raggedy Ann, "We haven't any fingers to cross!" Raggedy Ann had hardly said this than she stood upon her head.

"I don't care!" Raggedy Ann laughed, "For my head is stuffed with nice clean white cotton and it doesn't make me a bit dizzy! Really it is a lot of fun!"

When she said this, her feet came down to the ground and she wiggled one of her shoe button eyes at everybody. "You see," she smiled, "Whoever has the Magic Wishing Pebble is teasing us, and if they think we enjoy it, then they will quit, for they won't find any fun in it if we are having any fun! That's the way with selfish people. So if we always make them believe that their mischief does not annoy us, they will always let us be!"

CHAPTER NINE

WHEN Raggedy Ann and Raggedy Andy left the Muskrats and their neighbors, they walked down the bank of the Looking Glass Brook asking everyone they met if they knew who had found the Wishing Pebble which Raggedy Ann had buried in the sand.

"I don't know who has it!" Grampie Hoppytoad said, "But it must be a very magical pebble if it can bring lovely ice cream soda-water fountains by just wishing for them!"

"Oh, indeed, it is a very wonderful pebble!" Raggedy Andy replied. "Why Raggedy Ann only had it a few minutes and she wished for the ice cream soda-water fountain to be in the Muskrat living room and a lolly-pop garden to be at the Muskrat's kitchen door, and right away, there they were!"

"You know what I believe, Raggedy Andy?" asked Raggedy Ann.

"What?" Raggedy Andy asked in reply.

"Why, I believe that whoever it was who found the magical Wishing Pebble where I buried it, must have been watching us while we sat there in the sand. And I think that he heard me wish for the Lolly-pop garden, but he didn't hear me wish for the fountain. So, when he found the magical

Wishing Pebble he immediately wished that the Lolly-pop garden would grow near his own kitchen door!"

"And you think that he did not know about the Magical Ice Cream Soda-water Fountain?" asked Grampie Hoppytoad.

"That is what I believe!" said Raggedy Ann. "You see, Mister Muskrat wished all of his neighbors to share in the fun of drinking lovely ice cream sodas so he sent Freddie Fieldmouse to tell everybody. And I guess that whoever has the magical Wishing Pebble must have heard Freddie tell of the Soda-water Fountain."

"I hear every word you say!" a voice shouted across the Looking Glass Brook, at the three friends, "And I have the magical Wishing Pebble safe in my pocket and you will never, never get it, so there!"

"It seems to me that I have heard the voice before!" Grampie Hoppytoad said, "But I can't think who it is!"

"You'd better watch out, or I'll make you stand upon your head, Grampie Hoppytoad!" the voice cried.

"Why don't you do it now?" Grampie Hoppytoad shouted back across the Looking Glass Brook.

"You just wait and I will!" the voice replied, "I'm wishing it now and pretty soon you will stand right upon your head!"

"I feel 'kinda' funny!" said Grampie Hoppytoad to Raggedy Ann and Raggedy Andy.

"Quick! Cross your fingers!" said Raggedy Andy.

"No, I shan't!" said Grampie Hoppytoad, "I don't believe he can make me stand upon my head!"

"Can't I?" the voice shouted from the reeds across the Looking Glass Brook. "You just wait! I'm wishing real hard and you'll stand upon your head in a minute!"

"Ha! Ha! Ha!" laughed Grampie Hoppytoad, "I knew you couldn't do it! And I haven't got my fingers crossed either!"

"No wonder!" the voice cried, "I was holding the magical Wishing Pebble in my left hand! That's why! Now you just watch out! How does that feel to you now?"

JOHNNY GRUELLE

"I can't feel a thing!" laughed Grampie Hoppytoad, teasingly, "And I don't believe you really have the magical Wishing Pebble."

"Yes, I have!" the voice shouted, "For I have the lovely Ice Cream Soda-water Fountain in my own living room and the lolly-pop garden right at my own back door and no one shall have a single glass of ice cream soda water or a single lolly-pop from my lolly-pop garden!"

"I wouldn't be too sure of that!" cried Grampie Hoppy-toad, "For you can wish as hard as you like and you can't make me stand upon my head, so may be the magic has gone out of the Wishing Pebble and may be your magical Ice Cream Soda-water fountain and your lolly-pop garden has gone with it!" Grampie Hoppytoad winked his eye at Raggedy Ann, as if to say, "I'm just teasing!"

"Well! something is wrong with the magical Wishing Pebble!" cried the voice, "Because I've never had any trouble making anyone stand upon their heads when I wished it!"

"I'm going home and have a glass of ice cream soda-water and leave you there to think how nice it tastes!"

"Isn't he mean!" laughed Raggedy Ann, "But when a person grows stingy, it isn't very long before they lose all they have, and then, MY! how quick they are to ask favors of those they have been stingy with!"

"Yes," laughed Grampie Hoppytoad, "The best way to be is to do as many pleasant and kindly things as possible for others, then others love you and help you in return when you need it!"

* * * * *

"I'll keep my two large goggle eyes open for the person who has the magical Wishing Pebble!" said Grampie Hoppy-toad as he shook hands goodbye with Raggedy Ann and Raggedy Andy, "And if I find out who has it, I'll hunt you and tell you."

"Thank you very much!" said Raggedy Ann and Raggedy

Andy. "I believe some day we will find the magical Wishing Pebble and then we can have lots of fun wishing."

"Do you know what, Raggedy Ann?" asked Raggedy Andy, "I bet you that whoever has the magical Wishing Pebble can't make its wishes come true any more because they keep wishing unkind things!"

"I'll bet so too!" laughed Raggedy Ann, "And it wouldn't s'prise me a little teeny, weeny bit to find out that the magical ice cream soda-water fountain will not taste very good to whoever has the magical Wishing Pebble!"

"And the lolly-pops won't taste good to them either!" said Raggedy Andy.

"I can hear you talking about me!" cried the voice of whoever had the magical Wishing Pebble, "And you'd better be careful what you say!"

"Why don't you come out from behind those weeds so we can see you?" asked Raggedy Andy.

"Because!" the voice said angrily, "I went home and I found my magical ice cream soda-water fountain and my lolly-pop garden just as I left them."

"How did the soda-water taste?" asked Raggedy Andy.

"I didn't taste any!" the voice replied, "And I believe you two old rag dolls are the cause of my soda-water fountain tasting bitter and my lolly-pops tasting like burnt candy!"

"Why! We haven't anything to do with it!" said Raggedy Ann, "The magical Wishing Pebble worked very nice when I had it, and all the little creatures thought the ice cream sodas were so nice!"

"And I know just why it worked such nice magical things for Raggedy Ann!" the selfish person cried.

"I believe it will work just as well for you, if you wish unselfish things!" said Raggedy Ann.

"You can't fool me that way!" the selfish person cried, "I know that you have a candy heart, Raggedy Ann! And that is the reason you can work the magical Wishing Pebble so nice!"

"That isn't the reason at all!" laughed Raggedy Ann. "If you wish nice things you'll soon find that they come true!"

"You just wait!" cried the voice, "I'll show you! Just as soon as I catch Raggedy Ann asleep, I'll take her candy heart, then all my wishes will come true just the same as her's did!"

"You won't ever get Raggedy Ann's candy heart!" Raggedy Andy cried, "For I shall watch over her all the time she sleeps and if I ever catch you—"

"I'll see who you are!" cried Raggedy Andy as he ran and jumped into the Looking Glass Brook, intending to swim across and chase the disagreeable person. But when Raggedy Andy lit in the water, he kicked and splashed about and only succeeded in swimming in a circle.

Raggedy Ann got a long stick and as she fished Raggedy Andy out, she saw a queer little creature run out of the weeds on the other side of the Looking Glass Brook and go scampering away as fast as his thin legs would carry him.

Raggedy Andy was dripping wet, but he still wore his cheery smile.

"When you get nice and dry, Raggedy Andy, we'll start and follow the little man, for I saw which way he ran!" said Raggedy Ann.

And the two Raggedys sat in the warm sunshine and laughed as happily as they ever had before they lost the wonderful magical Wishing Pebble.

CHAPTER TEN

WHEN the nice warm sunshine had thoroughly dried Raggedy Andy after his splash in the Looking Glass Brook, the two dolls walked down the bank, looking for a place to cross.

After a while they came to a funny little hole in the bank and all about the hole the mud had been built up into a small wall about an inch high.

"Hm!" mused Raggedy Ann as she noticed the queer hole, "I wonder what that is?"

Raggedy Andy laid flat upon the ground and looked down into the hole.

"Can you see anything?" asked Raggedy Ann.

"I can't see a thing! Dear be! Sub thigs grabbed by dose ad I cad tog plaid!"

"Did you say, 'something grabbed your nose and you can't talk plain?' " laughed Raggedy Ann.

"Yes!" Raggedy Andy replied, still with his rag face over the hole, "Subthig is pinjig by dose!"

"Something pinching your nose?" Raggedy Ann repeated in surprise.

"Thad's whad I said, Raggedy Add!" Raggedy Andy laughed, "Bud I cad see whad id is! Id dode hurd a bid, though!"

"You talk just like you had a cold in your nose, Raggedy Andy!" Raggedy Ann could not help laughing. "Shall I pull you away from the hole? It may be a pinching bug!"

"I'm not a pinching bug!" a queer little voice said from down beneath Raggedy Andy's face.

"Id isn'd a pijjig bug!" laughed Raggedy Andy, "Id jusd said so!"

"I heard it!" laughed Raggedy Ann. "I guess it would be best if I pulled you away from the hole!" And with this, Raggedy Ann lifted Raggedy Andy away from the queer little hole and there, hanging on Raggedy Andy's painted nose was

Clifton Crawdad. Clifton Crawdad flapped his tail as hard as he could, but he did not let go of Raggedy Andy's painted nose.

Clifton Crawdad pinched Raggedy Andy's painted nose so hard it was all pinched up into a wrinkle and to keep from losing his hold, Clifton Crawdad reached up with his other claw and caught hold of Raggedy Andy's shoe-button eye.

"Here!" said Raggedy Ann reprovingly, "I wouldn't do that, Clifton Crawdad. You may scratch all the shinyness off Raggedy Andy's shoe-button eye!"

Clifton Crawdad only flapped his tail and, as he had water at the bottom of his queer little home, he splashed mud all around Raggedy Andy's chin.

"I guess I'll pick him off!" said Raggedy Ann, after thinking awhile. "He may get your necktie all muddy!"

"Maybe you had bedder pig hib off!" said Raggedy Andy, "Bud be careful you dode hurd hib!"

Raggedy Ann caught hold of Clifton Crawdad with her two soft rag hands, "Does that hurt you?" she asked in her kindest raggedy tone.

"No! not a tiny speck!" said Clifton Crawdad, "You see I have a very hard shell and your hands are nice and soft!"

Raggedy Ann pulled upon Clifton Crawdad until she held him out from Raggedy Andy's rag face and Clifton Crawdad's arms stretched up till Andy cried, "Waid a binnet, Raggedy Add, you musn'd pull his arbs off!"

"She won't pull my arms off!" said Clifton Crawdad, "For I'll let go before she pulls that hard!"

"Then you'd better let go!" suggested Raggedy Ann, "For I'm going to pull hard now!"

"Then I'll let go!" said Clifton Crawdad. And when he did let go, Raggedy Ann was pulling so hard, she fell over backwards, carrying Clifton Crawdad with her. Raggedy Ann put Clifton Crawdad down upon the sand and smoothed out her apron. "Just see how muddy you made Raggedy Andy's chin!" she said reprovingly.

"Raggedy Andy should never have put his face over my front door!" said Clifton Crawdad.

"Well, I'll wash it off before the mud dries," laughed Raggedy Andy.

"You might have lost one of your claws!" said Raggedy Ann.

"Yes!" said Raggedy Andy after he had washed his face, "What if I had been someone else and just picked you off in a hurry? I might have pulled one of your claws right off!"

"I know it!" Clifton Crawdad answered, "But after a while it would have grown on again!"

"I'm glad you didn't do it though, Raggedy Andy!"

"I always thought you Crawdads lived in the water!" said Raggedy Ann.

"We do most of the time!" Clifton Crawdad answered, "But sometimes we dig little round homes in the banks of the streams and live there!"

"Have you seen a queer little man with thin legs and a Wishing Pebble?" asked Raggedy Ann; and then she told Clifton Crawdad all about the Wishing Pebble and the Muskrat's ice cream soda water fountain. When she had finished telling him, Clifton Crawdad said, "I know who you mean, for one day he came here and filled my front door full of mud and it took me a long time to clean it out again! It's Minky, and he's very unkind and selfish! I didn't know he had a magical Wishing Pebble, though. You'd think that anyone with such a wonderful pebble would be very happy and kindly!"

"Indeed, he should be!" said Raggedy Ann.

"Well, if Minky ever puts his face down like Raggedy Andy did at my front door, I'll hold him until you come and take the pebble away from him!"

"No, you mustn't do that, Clifton Crawdad!" said Raggedy Ann, "For although it did not hurt Raggedy Andy when you pinched him, it would hurt Minky very much! And we must never hurt others even when they are mean to us!"

CHAPTER ELEVEN

"ISN'T it nice to sit here in the sunshine!" Raggedy Ann exclaimed, "It makes me feel so nice and sleepy!"

"It feels just as if I was getting so light and fluffy I could fly!" said Raggedy Andy as he laid back and put his arms under his rag head. "Put your head on me for a pillow, Raggedy Ann!" he said. "The sky is as blue as blue can be, and the clouds are as white as pop-corn. It's nice to lie here and look up at them!"

Raggedy Ann and Raggedy Andy dozed and had hardly been asleep five minutes when the grass beside them was parted and the two little eyes looked out at them.

"I wish I knew for sure whether they are asleep or not!" said Minky.

Minky was the selfish and disagreeable person who had found the magical Wishing Pebble when Raggedy Ann had buried it in the sand.

"I guess they are asleep for sure!" chuckled Minky as he crept out of the grass toward the sleeping Raggedys.

"I must get Raggedy Ann's candy heart!" he said out loud to himself, "Then if I eat the candy heart, I am sure that I can make the magical Wishing Pebble work.

And as Minky had by this time reached the sleeping Raggedys, he took a piece of string from his pocket and tied their rag hands to their bodies and tied their feet together; then he pushed sticks in the sand and tied their rag bodies to the sticks.

From his pocket Minky took a pair of scissors and was just about to snip a hole in Raggedy Ann's apron so that he could snip another hole in her rag body and get her candy heart when Raggedy Ann awakened.

"Ha! Ha! Ha!" laughed Minky, "I've got you tied tight! And I mean to have your candy heart!"

"It won't do you a speck of good!" laughed Raggedy Ann, "For it wasn't the candy heart that made the magical Wishing Pebble so magical!"

"Well, now I'll get it and we will soon see!" cried Minky, as

he came toward Raggedy Ann to snip a hole in her rag body.

Minky sat down beside Raggedy Ann to begin the snip, and had hardly got seated before he let out a howl and tried to get to his feet. "Wow!" he cried as tears streamed down his nose, "Something is biting me and won't let go! Wow! And turning over and over Minky rolled until he splashed into the Looking Glass Brook and came up kicking and squealing, wet and soaking. The selfish creature scrambled to the other side and went howling over the bank and into the bushes.

"There!" said Clifton Crawdad, "I am 'even' with Minky for filling my doorway with mud!"

"What's all the fuss about?" Raggedy Andy asked as he rubbed his shoe-button eyes sleepily.

Clifton Crawdad and Raggedy Ann told him about Minky.

"Well, I guess we had better walk down the side of the Looking Glass Brook until we find a place to cross!" said Raggedy Andy.

"Yes! I guess we had better go now!" Raggedy Ann agreed as she held out her hand to shake Clifton Crawdad's claw good-bye.

"Good-bye!" said Clifton Crawdad, as he held out his left claw.

"Why you must never shake hands left-handed!" said Raggedy Andy.

"I have to!" laughed Clifton Crawdad, "I left my right claw hanging on Mister Minky's pants! And I hope it is still pinching him to beat the band!"

"Oh dear!" Raggedy Ann cried, as she got on her hands

and knees beside Clifton Crawdad, "I am so sorry you lost your claw just for me! I would rather have had Minky get my candy heart many times than to have seen you hurt. You two wait here just a minute! I'll be right back!" and up the bank she scrambled and out across the yellow meadow.

At the first spider telegraph wire she came to, Raggedy Ann found Jenny Cricket calling up the grocery for her next day's dinner. When Jenny Cricket had finished with her marketing, Raggedy Ann asked, "Jenny Cricket, do you know how to telegraph the little gnome who works magic cures?"

"Yes, indeed!" Jenny Cricket replied.

It took Jennie Cricket only a moment to call Mister Gnome and he said he would be over in a few moments.

Raggedy Ann told Jennie Cricket all about the magical Wishing Pebble and selfish Mister Minky and all about how Clifton Crawdad lost his claw helping her and Raggedy Andy escape from Mister Minky.

"That was kind of Clifton Crawdad!" said Jenny Cricket. "Well here is Mister Gnome!"

Raggedy Ann lost no time in telling Mister Gnome about Clifton Crawdad and Mister Gnome lost no time in flying to the Looking Glass Brook, so by the time Raggedy Ann reached there, Mister Gnome had a new claw upon Clifton Crawdad and had hurried back home.

"Now we can shake hands good-bye with you, Clifton Crawdad!" laughed Raggedy Ann, "And thank you so much for helping Raggedy Andy and me!"

"Oh!" laughed Clifton Crawdad, "I am so glad that I could help you and I hope you can find the magical Wishing Pebble again!"

So Raggedy Ann and Raggedy Andy shook hands good-bye with Clifton Crawdad, and arm-in-arm, they walked down the bank, looking for a place to cross the Looking Glass Brook.

"Clifton Crawdad was an ugly little fellow!" said Raggedy Andy, "But he surely was a good friend to have when we needed one!"

CHAPTER TWELVE

"WELL!" Raggedy Andy said, "After this, Raggedy Ann, when you feel sleepy, I'll try and not feel sleepy at the same time! Because I do not want to be asleep when old Mister Minky comes snooping around trying to get your candy heart!"

"If it had not been for kind Clifton Crawdad, I guess Mister Minky would have had my candy heart. But it would not have been of any use to him!" laughed Raggedy Ann.

"Do you think you would be as kindly if you did not have a candy heart, Raggedy Ann?"

"Oh, yes, indeed!" Raggedy Ann replied, "It does not make any difference with either of us, Raggedy Andy! You are just as kindly as I am, and you have no candy heart!"

"That is true, Raggedy Ann!" Raggedy Andy said, "Perhaps it is the nice clean white cotton which we have in our rag heads!"

"Maybe it is!" Raggedy Ann agreed.

"Ha! Ha! Ha!" laughed a voice from a tree back of the two Raggedys, "I am glad to hear you say that!" And looking up, who should Raggedy Ann and Raggedy Andy see but old Mister Minky looking at them from the lower branches.

"I do believe he is going to fish!" said Raggedy Andy.

Mister Minky, from his perch in the tree let a line with the hook on it fall down amongst the tall grass at the bottom of the tree.

"How do you expect to catch any fish in the tall grass, Mister Minky?" Raggedy Ann asked.

"Oh, I'm not fishing for fish!" Mister Minky said with a sly wink.

"What do you s'pect he's fishing for Raggedy Andy?" whispered Raggedy Ann.

"Less go over and see!" Raggedy Andy whispered back to Raggedy Ann.

When Mister Minky saw the two Raggedys coming over to see what he was fishing for he almost fell off the limb, he

was so tickled, for Mister Minky was really fishing for Raggedy Ann and Raggedy Andy, although they did not know it. And Mister Minky wished to get the two rag dolls underneath the tree, so he could jerk upon the line and catch the hook in their clothing and pull them up to the limb. So the Raggedys, not knowing what Mister Minky intended doing, walked right over under the tree and looked in the grass to see what Mister Minky was fishing for.

"He! He! He!" Minky chuckled as he gave his line a jerk.

"Dear me Suzz!" Raggedy Ann cried. Mister Minky's hook had caught in Raggedy Ann's apron and then in Raggedy Andy's pants, and there the two rag dolls hung in the air, twisting and twirling about as Mister Minky hauled them up to the limb.

"Now I told you I was glad to hear you say it was the

nice clean white cotton in your heads that made the wishes come true!"

"We didn't say that!" cried Raggedy Andy, "We said that it only made us kindly!"

"You can't fool me!" Mister Minky replied, "So I will pull you up to the limb here and tie you tight, then I'll take Raggedy Ann's candy heart and all the cotton out of your rag heads! Whee! Won't I have fun then!"

"No, indeed, you will not have fun!" Raggedy Ann said, as she wiggled and kicked, "For no one can have fun with anything they take from another, and you will find that instead of making your wishes come true, it will keep your wishes from coming true!"

"We'll soon see about that!" shouted Minky, as he reached into his pocket for his scissors so that he could snip a hole in Raggedy Ann's dress and get her candy heart. But Mister Minky evidently did not see Bertha Bumblebee sitting upon the tree trunk right behind him.

"I guess you'd better not snip Raggedy Ann's dress today!" said Bertha Bumblebee very buzzy-like. And with that, she flew and gave Mister Minky such a pop upon the top of his little round head he let out a great cry and tumbled right out of the tree and Raggedy Ann and Raggedy Andy fell right on top of him. Mister Minky got to his feet as quickly as he could, and without looking behind him to see what had happened, ran across the great yellow meadow, holding his hand to the place where Bertha Bumblebee hadpopped him.

It took Raggedy Ann and Raggedy Andy only a moment to get the hook out of their clothes.

"Isn't it funny," said Raggedy Ann, "That when we try to get fun from injuring another, trouble always bounces up and hits us a pop and we get fooled every time!"

And Bertha Bumblebee winked her eye at Raggedy Ann and flew out across the Looking Glass Brook, singing a loud buzzy tune as she went.

CHAPTER THIRTEEN

RAGGEDY ANN and Raggedy Andy went skipping along the shore of the Looking Glass Brook, stopping here and there to lift up the head of a pretty little flower, "To see if there are any Fairies sleeping inside," said Raggedy Ann. They were careful each time they looked into a flower not to "jiggle" it too much and awaken the little Fairy. And when they found a little, teeny weeny Fairy, sound asleep inside a pretty little flower, Raggedy Ann's and Raggedy Andy's little shoe-button eyes twinkled with excitement and fun.

The two rag dolls strolled along until they came to a log which had fallen across the Looking Glass Brook, forming a nice bridge over which they could walk and get upon the side of the brook where Mister Minky lived.

"I guess the best thing for us to do," said Raggedy Ann, "is to try and get the Wishing Pebble away from Minky and then we can wish him to be real kind and loving!"

"Yes!" agreed Raggedy Andy, "That would be a good plan! For, while old Mister Minky has the Wishing Pebble, no one gets any good out of it, and if we can get it and wish Mister Minky to be real good and generous, then we can give the Wishing Pebble back to him and he will have lots of fun wishing nice things for others!"

"Then let's cross the brook upon this log!" said Raggedy Ann, "And we will try and find Mister Minky and ask him for the Wishing Pebble!"

Raggedy Ann and Raggedy Andy had just reached the center of the log bridge when their feet slipped out from under them and they both went "splash" into the Looking Glass Brook and as they looked up, who should they see coming out upon the log with a long stick in his hand but Mister Minky.

"That's the time I fooled you!" he shouted as the Raggedys splashed about in the water. "I thought you would try to cross here and I put soap suds upon the log and made it slippery so that you would slip and fall into the water. Now

I will fish you out with this long stick and drag you to the bank and get Raggedy Ann's candy heart!"

Mister Minky reached out with the long stick and poked at Raggedy Ann, trying to get the end of the stick fastened in her dress or apron, but each time Mister Minky thought he had Raggedy Ann's dress fastened upon the stick, Raggedy Andy gave Raggedy Ann a pull and the stick came loose.

"If you don't quit loosening Raggedy Ann's dress when I get the stick fastened in it, I'll tie a stone around your neck when I fish you out, Raggedy Andy, then I'll throw you back into the water and you'll sink!"

"Ha Ha Ha!" laughed Raggedy Andy, "That wouldn't hurt me a speck, Mister Minky! And you might as well know now, that you will never get Raggedy Ann's candy heart if I can help it."

"Dear me!" Raggedy Ann said, "To hear you talk, Mister Minky, one would think Raggedy Andy had done something mean to you!"

"I don't care!" Mister Minky replied, "I am tired of having Raggedy Andy keep me from getting your candy heart and having my wishes come true!"

"If you would just let us take the Magic Wishing Pebble for a few minutes we would wish something nice for you and you would then be able to make the loveliest wishes and have them all come true!"

"I wouldn't trust you with the Magic Wishing Pebble, for I know you would wish something very unpleasant for me!" said the selfish little creature. "I'll fish Raggedy Andy out first and tie the stone about his neck! Ha Ha!" he cried as his long stick caught in Raggedy Andy's pants, "Now I have you!" And with many winks and chuckles, Mister Minky drew Raggedy Andy up to the log. Raggedy Ann kicked and splashed about in the water trying to swim to Raggedy Andy and pull him from the stick, but Raggedy Andy did not even wiggle as Mister Minky pulled him up on the log.

"Now for a large stone!" Minky cried, and leaving Raggedy Andy laying across the log, Minky ran ashore and came back carrying a large stone and a piece of string. But just as Mister Minky ran out to where Raggedy Andy lay across the log, Minky's feet flew out from under him and with a cry and a splash he fell into the Looking Glass Brook. "Ha! Ha! Ha!" laughed Raggedy Andy as he got to his feet and was careful not to step upon the soap sudsy place on the log. "That's the time you got fooled, Mister Minky! For I moved back over the slippery place on the log when your back was turned and you came running right out upon the soap suds!" It took Raggedy Andy only a moment to pull Raggedy Ann ashore and then by putting sand upon the log where the soap suds had been, the two rag dolls crossed the log in safety.

"Shall we pull Minky out of the water?" Raggedy Andy asked, as the two rag dolls looked back and saw the naughty little fellow kicking about.

Raggedy Ann nodded her head and Andy soon reached Mister Minky with the long stick and pulled him ashore.

"You just wait until I catch you the next time!" Minky shook his fists and shouted as he ran through the weeds.

Raggedy Ann and Raggedy Andy laughed softly to themselves and followed the wet trail Minky left on the ground.

"I'm glad that we can make our troubles lighter by laughing at them!" smiled Raggedy Ann.

CHAPTER FOURTEEN

"WHERE in the world are you Raggedys going?" Winnie Woodchuck asked, as she stepped out in the path in front of Raggedy Ann and Raggedy Andy.

Then seeing that the two were soaking wet, Winnie Woodchuck shook her head. "My! My! Land sakes, Raggedy Ann and Raggedy Andy, your clothes are soaking wet, you must come right home with me and let me get you dry ones!"

Walter Woodchuck was sitting upon the front steps smoking a pipeful of mullein leaves, for someone had told him mullein leaves were good for hug-tite-iss, whatever that may be.

"Oh goody!" Walter cried, as he knocked the ashes from his pipe, "I was just wishing Winnie would bring someone home with her! We haven't had visitors for almost two hours! Come right in!"

Winnie Woodchuck hurried and got some nice dry clothes for Raggedy Ann and Raggedy Andy, and Walter Woodchuck made a fire in the fire-place so the Raggedys could get their feet dry. You know, both Raggedy Ann and Raggedy Andy's shoes were just sewed upon their feet and there was no way of taking off their shoes without spoiling them.

The little fire of birch bark sputtered and crackled merrily and in a few minutes the Raggedys were just as nice and dry as could be.

"Now we will have some licorice-root tea," Winnie Woodchuck said as she brought in a tray of tea cups and Woodchuck cookies, "for I know how hungry you must be after falling in the brook!"

So Winnie and Walter Woodchuck and Raggedy Ann and Raggedy Andy sat in front of the little crackly fire and drank the licorice-root tea and it was ever so nice and did not make the cotton stuffing in the Raggedys the least bit damp, 'cause it was made so nicely.

And, while they sat drinking the nice licorice-root tea, the door opened and without even knocking the teeny weeniest knock, in walked Minky.

"I just guess I'll have a cup of that licorice-root tea!" he said.

Now, everyone knows that the Woodchucks are very friendly little folk and when they find anyone in trouble they are always ready to help them, but when Minkie came stomping into their nice, clean Woodchuck living-room with his muddy feet and without knocking, Winnie Woodchuck did not like it!

"Now you just march right out, Mister Minkie!" she said, "You are very rude!"

"Ha, ha, ha! You'd better be very careful how you call me rude, Winnie Woodchuck!" Minkie said, "I 'spect you don't know that I have a very magical Wishing Pebble and I can work magic on you!"

"The Wishing Pebble doesn't work for him at all!" Raggedy Andy told Winnie and Walter Woodchuck, "And the reason it doesn't work magic for him is because he always tries to do selfish things!"

"Just you wait until I catch you alone, Raggedy Andy!" Minkie shouted, much louder than was necessary, "Just you wait, that's what!"

"Well," Winnie Woodchuck said, as she ran to the kitchen and came back with her broom, "Magic Wishing Pebble or

not, you can not stay here and spoil our nice little party, Mister Minkie!" and she paddy-whacked the mean little fellow so hard with the broom he was glad to dash out of the door.

"Now then, just for that I shall change you all into monkeys with my Wishing Pebble!" Minkie cried, as he shook his fist in the door.

"And I 'spect I shall rassel you and take the Wishing Pebble away from you!" Raggedy Andy said as he ran toward Minkie.

My! how they tusseled! This way and that! First Minkie tried to put his foot behind Raggedy Andy and trip him, then Raggedy Andy tried to put his foot behind Minkie and trip him, but neither one could throw the other. Finally Minkie grew very angry and, catching hold of Raggedy Andy's pretty collar, he tore it from Raggedy Andy's nice striped shirt.

"Anyway, even if you did tear my nice pretty shirt, I shall not tear your coat!" Raggedy Andy said, "For it is wrong to destroy anything! But I shall rassel you much harder now!" And sure enough Raggedy Andy did. He just rasseled twice as hard, and the first thing Minkie knew, he had tumbled upon his back and Raggedy Andy was on top.

"Aha! Aha! Mister Minkie! Now will you be good?" Walter Woodchuck cried as he danced about Minkie and Raggedy Andy, "Now take the magical Wishing Pebble away from him, Raggedy Andy!"

"Oh no!" Raggedy Ann cried, "It would be wrong for Raggedy Andy to take the Wishing Pebble from Minkie! That would break all the magic of the Pebble, and besides, it is wrong to do anything like that!"

"Then I shan't take away the Wishing Pebble!" Raggedy Andy said as he got to his feet and helped Minkie get up.

"Ha! I guess you won't take it away from me!" Minkie said, "It is home!" and before Raggedy Andy could jump to one side, Minkie gave him a push and sent Raggedy Andy flying head over heels.

Then Minkie ran home as fast as he could scamper, laughing as if he had played a good joke on Raggedy Andy.

"Don't you care!" Walter and Winnie Woodchuck said as they helped Raggedy Andy stand up and brushed the leaves from his clothes, "Minkie is a very, very, very rude little fellow, and someday, I'll bet he will be sorry!"

Winnie Woodchuck got out her sewing box and in a few minutes she sewed Raggedy Andy's collar on his pretty striped shirt just a good as new. "I 'spect if you only had the wonderful Wishing Pebble, you would make some nice wishes!" Winnie Woodchuck said to Raggedy Ann.

"You bet she would, Winnie Woodchuck!" Raggedy Andy answered, "When Raggedy Ann had the Wishing Pebble before, she wished for the nicest things in the Muskrat house, but she lost the Pebble and as soon as Mister Minkie got it, he wished for the ice-cream soda-water fountain and the patch of lollypops to disappear, so now the kindly Muskrats have no soda fountain in their front room!"

"Hmm," Walter Woodchuck mused, as he rubbed his chin, "I 'spect I'll be back in a few minutes, Raggedy Ann and Raggedy Andy!" he said. "Please excuse me!"

"Yes, indeed!" the Raggedys said as Walter Woodchuck went out the door.

"I 'spect maybe, speaking of ice cream sodas made Walter Woodchuck hungry for candy!" Winnie Woodchuck chuckled, "Maybe he has gone to the store to buy some candy!" So she got out a roly poly game and she and the Raggedys sat on the floor in front of the crackly fire and played with the game while they waited for Walter Woodchuck to return.

CHAPTER FIFTEEN

AS SOON as Walter Woodchuck got outside his front door, he winked both little brown eyes at a tree and said to himself, "If old Mister Minkie was mean enough to get the nice magical Wishing Pebble and wish all the nice things to disappear from the kind Muskrat home, after Raggedy Ann had given the things to them, I believe someone should borrow the magical Wishing Pebble from selfish old Mister Minkie!" And Walter Woodchuck winked again at another tree and smiled to himself. "So I shall just walk over to Mister Minkie's house and borrow the Wishing Pebble from him!" And he chuckled his soft Woodchuck chuckle as he walked along.

Walter Woodchuck knew just where old Mister Minkie lived and in a few minutes he was knocking at the door.

"Who is knocking at my door?" Minkie shouted in a growly voice.

"It's Walter Woodchuck, and I have come to see you!" Walter Woodchuck replied.

"Then you can run right smack dab back home!" Minkie shouted, "I shall not let you in!"

"Then you come out!" Walter said.

"I shan't do it!" Mister Minkie said, "And if you don run home right away, you'll be sorry, that's what!"

"Ha! What will you do? Just you tell me that, Mister Minkie! What will you do?" Walter Woodchuck asked.

Minkie did not reply, and he was so quiet Walter thought surely Mister Minkie must have gone to sleep, but the first thing he knew he was lifted clear off his feet and jerked up in the air.

"Ha! That's the time I fooled you, Walter Woodchuck!" Minkie shouted as he pulled and pulled on the rope until Walter Woodchuck was almost as high as the roof of Minkie's house. "Now I shall fasten the end of the rope to the chimney and you can just hang there!"

So the mean creature tied the end of the rope to the chimney and left poor Walter Woodchuck hanging against the side of the house.

Walter Woodchuck wiggled and twisted and kicked this way and that, but he could not get loose. Minkie had fastened a hook in the end of the rope and had caught the hook in Walter Woodchuck's suspenders in back, and of course, Walter could not reach around there and unfasten it.

"I wonder what Winnie Woodchuck will think when I do not return?" Walter Woodchuck thought to himself.

While Walter was wondering this, Winnie Woodchuck was wondering why Walter did not return from the store with the candy she thought he had gone for. "Maybe Walter Woodchuck stopped to visit with someone along the way!" Raggedy Ann suggested when Winnie spoke of it.

"Oh no!" Winnie Woodchuck replied, "Walter always hurries right home from the store. I 'spect I will run down the path and meet him!"

So Winnie Woodchuck went down the path and pretty soon she met Wallace Woodpecker. Wallace Woodpecker was the mail carrier in the deep, deep woods and knew all the news.

"Have you seen Walter Woodchuck?" Winnie asked.

"Yesir!" Wallace Woodpecker replied, "He is down at Mister Minkie's house. At least, he was going that way when I saw him. But I'll tell you one thing, Winnie, if I were you, I wouldn't let Walter Woodchuck go to see Mister Minkie very often 'cause Mister Minkie is a disagreeable creature!"

"Indeed! He is!" Winnie agreed. Then she thanked Wallace Woodpecker and ran down to Mister Minkie's house. And when she saw Walter hanging by his suspender to the hook at the end of the rope, Winnie was very angry.

She knew in a moment that Minkie had played a trick on Walter, so she went and thumped upon Minkie's door, "THUMP! THUMP! THUMP!" like that, only a great deal louder. "Come in!" Minkie called through the door.

So Winnie Woodchuck walked into Minkie's house, intending to give Mister Minkie a great piece of her mind, but she had hardly opened the door before Minkie caught her and had her tied to a chair. "Now, I 'spect you won't say much," he said. Then when he saw that Winnie Woodchuck did intend saying a great deal he stuffed a large hanky in her mouth so she couldn't talk.

"Ha, ha, ha!" Minkie laughed, "Pretty soon I'll bet a nickel Raggedy Ann and Raggedy Andy will come to hunt you, and I shall capture them as easy as I did you and Walter."

CHAPTER SIXTEEN

RAGGEDY ANN and Raggedy Andy sat upon the floor in the Woodchuck home and played with the roly poly game for a long time. First Ann won the game then Raggedy Andy won the game. "Isn't it time Winnie Woodchuck returned?" Raggedy Ann asked.

"Maybe we had better go see what can be keeping the Woodchucks so long!" Raggedy Andy replied, "Maybe they have caught their feet in a trap!"

"Oh no, Raggedy Andy," Raggedy Ann said, "There are no traps in this deep, deep woods, I am certain! There are too many cunning little gnomes and elves and fairies living here. And you know," she added, "They watch out for the other little woodland creatures!"

So Raggedy Ann put away the roly poly game and she and Raggedy Andy ran down the path through the woods until they came to Minkie's home; there they saw Walter Woodchuck hanging way up in the air near the house top.

"Aha!" Raggedy Ann said, "I'll bet Minkie did that! Let us ask Walter Woodchuck." "Yes it was Minkie!" Walter Woodchuck said when Raggedy Andy asked him who had pulled him up there, "And," Walter said, "Winnie Woodchuck came to rescue me and I am certain the Minkie has captured her, for she hasn't come out of the house and I am sure she went in the side door!"

"Dear me!" Raggedy Ann said, "What shall we do, Raggedy Andy?"

Raggedy Andy took off his cap and scratched his head with a little stick, but he could not think of anything to do. "Unless I go inside and rassel Minky!" he finally said.

"Yes! And have him capture you too? Indeed! You shall not go inside Minkie's house until we find out just what he has done with poor Winnie Woodchuck!"

So the Raggedys slipped up to one of Minkie's windows and peeped inside. There they saw poor Winnie Woodchuck

tied fast to a chair and she wiggled and twisted trying to get loose.

"We must plan some way to rescue Walter Woodchuck first!" Raggedy Ann said, "Then we will plan a way to rescue Winnie Woodchuck next!"

"I'll tell you what less do!" Raggedy Andy said, "I'll pretend that I am returning to the Woodchuck house and you can pretend that you are going inside Minkie's house. Then I will run around to Minkie's back door, while you talk to Minkie at the front door. If I can run inside, I will untie Winnie Woodchuck and then we will run out."

So Raggedy Ann and Raggedy Andy did just as Raggedy Andy had suggested and when Raggedy Ann came walking up to his door, Minkie said to himself, "Ha! Goody! Here comes Raggedy Ann all by herself! Now I can capture her and take her candy heart, then I am sure my magic Wishing Pebble will work!" And he waited for Raggedy Ann to knock upon the door.

Raggedy Ann thought to herself, "Maybe Minkie is hiding right behind the door just waiting for me." So she knocked upon the door and then had to smile to herself, for as soon as she knocked Minkie said, "Come in, Raggedy Ann!" and Raggedy Ann knew Minkie had been watching her all the time.

"I 'spect I shall not come in today, Mister Minkie," Raggedy Ann replied, "You must open the door, I wish to talk with you." So Minkie opened the door and poked his long nose out. "What do you wish to say, Raggedy Ann?" he asked.

"Hmm! Le'ss see!" Raggedy Ann mused. "Oh yes! I remember now Mister Minkie, I want to ask you something. Did you ever hear of 'Slapwinkies?' "

"Why! What a silly thing!" Minkie said. "Of course not! What are 'Slapwinkies' Raggedy Ann!"

"Why!" Raggedy Ann replied, as if greatly surprised, "If you would only come out here and look in the grass, you might see a Slapwinkie; who knows?"

"If you are trying to fool me, Raggedy Ann, you'll be mighty sorry!" Minkie said, as he opened the door and stepped out, "I should like very much to see one though!" and he closed the door behind him.

Then Raggedy Ann began singing a song just as loud as she could, for she knew by this time Raggedy Andy must be inside Minkie's house and she did not wish Minkie to hear Raggedy Andy.

And while Minkie was looking in the grass, Raggedy Andy had quietly sneaked into the house, untied Winnie Woodchuck and the two had slipped out the back door again and over into the bushes where they were hidden. Then Raggedy Andy told Winnie Woodchuck, "Now you stay hidden here in the bushes, Winnie, and I will run up the path toward Minkie and he will never know but that I have just come from your house. You must keep very quiet though and not let Minkie see you!"

So Raggedy Andy ran away and then came running up the path to where Minkie and Raggedy Ann were looking for Slapwinkies in the grass.

"Now what are you looking for, Mister Minkie?" Raggedy Andy asked very politely.

"I'm looking for Slapwinkies!" Minkie gruffly replied.

"Hmm!" Raggedy Andy said, "I never heard of Slapwinkies!"

"Then I'll bet Raggedy Ann was fooling me!" Minkie howled as he jumped to his feet. "I 'spect I will capture Raggedy Ann and take her candy heart, then my Wishing Pebble will work nicely!"

And he started as if he would catch Raggedy Ann, but Raggedy Andy said, "Wait, Mister Minkie! I 'spect if you would run up to Winnie Woodchuck's house and ask her, she would tell you if she has ever seen a Slapwinkie!"

"Ha!" Minkie laughed, forgetting himself, "Winnie Woodchuck isn't at home, so there!"

"Oh, is that so?" Raggedy Andy asked, "Why I just left Winnie Woodchuck not two minutes ago!"

Minkie looked queerly at Raggedy Andy and then ran into his house and out again. "She's escaped!" he cried. "How did she get away when I had her tied to a chair?"

Raggedy Ann and Raggedy Andy did not reply, for they did not wish to tell, but Raggedy Ann said, "I 'spect that Winnie Woodchuck escaped just like Walter Woodchuck will escape if you do not hurry and let him down yourself."

"There must be a lot of magic going on around here," Minkie said, "And for fear some of the magic will be worked on me before I get the Wishing Pebble working properly, I will untie the rope and let Walter down." So he ran indoors, up the stairway to the attic and then to the roof and let Walter down to the ground.

Raggedy Ann and Raggedy Andy and Walter Woodchuck walked away, never saying a word in reply to Minkie, and when they came to Winnie Woodchuck, they all caught hold of hands and ran toward the Woodchuck home, laughing heartily at the way they had played a good trick on old Mister Minkie.

CHAPTER SEVENTEEN

WHEN Raggedy Ann and Raggedy Andy left the Woodchuck home, they walked down the path toward Minkie's house, for they wished if they could, to get the fine Wishing Pebble so that they could make some lovely wishes and have the ice cream soda fountain in the living room of the Muskrats' cheery home.

And when they reached Minkie's home, there was a sign on the door which read, "Gone fishing for the day!"

"Less go to where he is fishing!" Raggedy Andy said to Raggedy Ann.

"That is a good plan!" Raggedy Ann agreed, as she started toward the stream where she knew Minkie had gone.

When they came to the stream, there upon a log sat Minkie fishing away for dear life.

"Have you caught anything?" Raggedy Andy asked.

"No sir!" Minkie replied, "I haven't even had a single bite!"

Just as he said this, Minkie's pole gave a big jerk and before he could catch himself, the little fellow was pulled from the log and went splashing into the water below. Raggedy Ann thought he would never come to the top again, for the water was so deep, but finally Minkie came to the surface and he was blowing and puffing to catch his breath.

Raggedy Andy got a long stick and held it out so Minkie could catch hold of it. Then Raggedy Andy with Raggedy Ann's aid, pulled until Minkie came ashore, all dripping wet.

"That settles it!" Minkie said when he could get his breath.

"Settles what?" Raggedy Andy asked.

"I shall never try to capture Raggedy Ann!" Minkie said, "I know now that both of you Raggedys are nice kind folks, and it was very wrong of me to take Raggedy Ann's lovely Wishing Pebble and make the ice-cream soda-water fountain disappear from the home of the Muskrats."

Raggedy Ann looked from Minkie to Raggedy Andy and smiled. It pleased her to think that Minkie had changed from

a mean little creature to a good little creature, and Raggedy Ann's shoe-button eyes wiggled with happiness.

"Yes sir, Raggedy Andy," Minkie said, "I am so very, very, very, very—" But Minkie could say no more for his eyes filled with tears again and he began crying loudly.

Raggedy Ann wiped the tears from Minkie's eyes, and when he had stopped weeping she said, "Do not feel so sad, Mister Minkie, if you will get the magical Wishing Pebble, I am certain in a few moments we can wish for the nice ice-cream

soda-water fountain to return to the Muskrats home and we can make them a lollypop garden and wish a whole lot of nice things for them. Then we can go down to their house and I am sure they will be glad to have you share in their pleasures!"

"Oh! Do you really believe they would do that, after the mean trick I played on them?" Minkie asked. Then when Raggedy Ann and Raggedy Andy told him, "Yes, indeed," Minkie said, "Then I shall run right home and get the Wishing Pebble, for I have it in a tea-cup up on the top shelf in my cupboard. I will be right back and I shall give it to you and let you make the nice wishes!"

So Raggedy Ann and Raggedy Andy sat down on a little log and twiggled their thumbs and waited for Minkie to return with the Wishing Pebble.

When they had waited a long, long time, Raggedy Andy said, "I wonder why Minkie doesn't return with the Wishing Pebble?"

"Maybe he has gone to sleep!" Raggedy Ann said in reply, "Let us walk to Minkie's house and see."

So the two dolls caught hold of hands and went trippity-trip down the path to Minkie's house. The front door stood wide open and after knocking, Raggedy Ann and Raggedy Andy went inside. There they found the furniture all turned topsy-turvey and the back door standing wide open.

Many dishes were broken and lay scattered about the floor. "I 'spect something has been going on here, like a fight, or a scuffle!" Raggedy Andy said. "See how the chairs are topsy-turvey and everything broken!"

Raggedy Ann agreed with Raggedy Andy. "Yes," she said, "Minkie has had a fight with someone sure pop!"

"And Minkie has chased whoever it was, right out of the back door!" Raggedy Andy called from the back porch. "Let's follow down through the woods; we can follow their tracks through the grass where they have trod it down!"

So, with Raggedy Andy in the lead, the two rag dolls ran as fast as they could in the direction the trail led.

In a few minutes Raggedy Ann and Raggedy Andy saw Minkie coming towards them and he was crying as hard as he could. "Why, Minkie!" Raggedy Ann exclaimed, "Whatever in the world has happened? Your clothes are torn and all muddy!"

So Minkie sat down on a stone and wiped the tears from his eyes. Then he looked sadly from Raggedy Ann to Raggedy Andy and said, "The magical Wishing Pebble is gone, Raggedy Ann and Raggedy Andy, and we shall never get it again to make nice wishes with."

"Why! Minkie!" Raggedy Andy said, "Who has it?"

"Bertram Bear!" Minkie replied. "When I left you, I ran home just as fast as I could, for I wanted Raggedy Ann to have her Wishing Pebble as soon as I could get it, but when I was running up the path near my house, I saw Bertram Bear come dashing out of the bushes and go running right into my front door. 'Hey! Bertram Bear,' I shouted, 'don't go into my house!' but into the house he went just the same, and of course I followed. And what do you think, Raggedy Ann and Raggedy Andy, there was Bertram Bear climbing up on a chair after the cup which held the Wishing Pebble. I knew than that Bertram Bear had listened to us talking back there in the woods and that he intended having the Wishing Pebble, so just as Bertram Bear jumped from the chair, I caught him and tried to take the Wishing Pebble away from him. We tusseled this way and that and upset all the furniture and all the dishes. But Bertram Bear finally pushed me over a chair and when I got to my feet, the mean creature was running out of the back door, and he has the Wishing Pebble in his pocket, for I saw him put it there!"

"Dear me!" was all Raggedy Andy could think of to say, but Raggedy Ann said, "Well, never mind, Mister Minkie! You run home and change your clothing and wash the mud from your face. Raggedy Andy and I will go to Bertram Bear's house and tell his mama how naughty he has been and you can follow us there! I 'spect Bertram Bear's mama will

make him return the Wishing Pebble mighty quick!"

So Minkie went sadly home, while Raggedy Ann and Raggedy Andy went toward the home of Bertram Bear.

CHAPTER EIGHTEEN

THE Bears lived high up on a hill in the deep, deep woods where the ground was very stony and there were great bowlders as large as chicken coops. Raggedy Ann and Raggedy Andy had never been there, but they could follow Bertram Bear's trail through the grass until they came to the stony ground and from there they could see the home of the Bears.

So Raggedy Ann and Raggedy Andy followed the path up the hill, in and around the large bowlders until they came to the home of Mrs. Bolivar Bear, and they knocked upon the door with their cotton-stuffed hands, "thump, thump, thump!"

Mrs. Bolivar Bear came to the door. "Why!" she cried, "It's two rag dolls! And they are alive!"

"May we come in, Mrs. Bolivar Bear?" Raggedy Ann asked.

"Certainly!" Mrs. Bolivar Bear replied, as she held the door open, but she wondered what two little rag dolls could be doing way up at her house.

"We were just having some nice ice cream soda-water!" Mrs. Bolivar Bear said, as she led the way into the dining-room to where Daddy Bolivar Bear and Bertram Bear sat near a sizzling soda-water fountain.

Mrs. Bolivar Bear brought Raggedy Ann and Raggedy Andy each a glass of ice cream soda-water and told them to sit down. "Bertram just made the soda fountain with a magical charm he found!" Mrs. Bolivar Bear said.

Of course, Bertram Bear knew right away that Raggedy Ann and Andy had come for the Wishing Pebble, for he had heard them talking about it with Minkie, and knew that the Wishing Pebble really belonged to Raggedy Ann, so he thought, "I must think of some way to fool Raggedy Ann and Raggedy Andy so that they can not tell my nice mama! What are you two rag dolls doing way up here amongst the rocks?" he asked Raggedy Ann.

Raggedy Ann tried to speak, but she could not say one word. "Why! how funny!" she thought, "I can think just as well as ever, but I can't talk even a smidge."

Then Bertram Bear turned to Raggedy Andy and said, "Didn't you get tired climbing up this high?" And Raggedy Andy tried to answer Bertram Bear but like Raggedy Ann, he could not speak one word.

"They could talk very well awhile ago!" Mrs. Boliver Bear said. "Something must have happened to their clock-work insides!"

She did not know that Raggedy Ann and Raggedy Andy were just stuffed with nice white cotton and their bodies had no clock-work.

"I 'spect I will take Raggedy Ann and Raggedy Andy out to the work-shed and fix their clock-work!" Bertram Bear said. "Maybe it just needs some oil." But to himself he said, "I will take the Raggedys out and throw them as far as I can from the highest rock, so that they will not come back again." So Bertram Bear picked up Raggedy Ann and Raggedy Andy and carried them out of the house and neither of the Raggedys could say even one word.

When he had gone far enough from the house so his mama and daddy could not hear him, he said, "Now I shall tell you just what I intend doing with you! I shall throw you both away and when you hit upon the ground way down below, you must run home as fast as you can, or the next time I will treat you far worse!"

And when the Raggedys did not reply, Bertram Bear and daddy can not hear you from here!"

And of course then the Raggedys could talk, and Raggedy Ann said, "You should feel so ashamed of yourself, Bertram Bear! You told your nice mama and daddy the biggest fib about the magical Wishing Pebble and I am sure the Wishing Pebble will not work for you when you tell fibs, or do anything wrong!"

"Ha, ha, ha!" Bertram Bear laughed, "Don't you believe it, Raggedy Ann! Didn't you see how my mama and daddy liked the nice soda-water? Now I shall throw you from this high stone and you had better never come back." And the mean Bear swung the Raggedys around his head and threw them just as far as he could.

Bertram Bear turned and walked back into the house, but the Raggedys just laid where they had fallen. Not that the fall had hurt them at all, but because they were lying side by side and wanted to think just what to do.

"Isn't he a mean Bear?" Raggedy Andy said. "How nice it is, that all creatures are not like Bertram Bear!"

"Oh!" Raggedy Ann said, as she sat up and smoothed out her yarn hair, "We will let Bertram Bear keep the magical Wishing Pebble, for it will not be magical very long."

The two Raggedys caught hold of hands and walked down the hill the way they had come and talked of the Wishing Pebble as they went along, then when they came to a bend in the path, there sat Freddy Fox upon a log and he was all out of breath from running.

"Why have you been running, Freddy Fox?" Raggedy Ann asked, as she came up to him.

Freddy Fox squinted his eyes until they were just tiny slits and smiled. "Oh!" he said, "Sometimes I just like to run and run and run, Raggedy Ann." But in his mind Freddy Fox was thinking, I must find out from Raggedy Ann and Raggedy Andy all I can about this wonderful Wishing Pebble I heard them talking of back there.

"Oh, yes!" Freddy Fox went on, "I run and run and run to keep in practice, so if anything chases me I can get away. But I wish I had a fine Wishing Stick or a magic ring so that I could make nice wishes and never have anything chase me!"

"It would be nice if you had one!" Raggedy Ann said. "Once I found a Wishing Pebble!" And she told Freddy Fox all about Minkie and how now Bertram Bear had it, but she did not tell how they were not able to work magic with it after they had it awhile.

So Freddy Fox said, "Well, I guess I shall never own one, so it is no use wishing for one." And with that, he bounced up and dashed away through the woods.

"Isn't he a strange creature!" Raggedy Ann said. "He did not look into our eyes when he talked to us, and you can never trust anyone who cannot look into your eyes when they speak to you!"

CHAPTER NINETEEN

"RAGGEDY ANN and Raggedy Andy are such silly things!" Freddy Fox said to himself as he left the two and ran away through the woods. "But then, Raggedy Ann and Raggedy Andy are only two old rag dolls and their heads are just stuffed with cotton; no one could expect them to be as smart and cunning as I am." And Freddy Fox made a turn in the woods and circled until he was headed up the hill toward the home of Bertram Bear.

"Bertram Bear is a silly thing, too!" Freddy Fox thought, "And it will be very easy for me to fool him and get the magical Wishing Pebble away from him; then I shall wish for everything I can think of, and I will not give anyone a single thing! Oh! I shall easily fool Bertram Bear! Just as easily as I fooled the Raggedys!"

And up he went and called outside Bertram's house, "Oh, Bertram Bear! Oh, Bertram Bear, come out!"

So Bertram Bear came out when he heard Freddy Fox, for often they had lots of fun together, though Freddy Fox always teased Bertram Bear a great deal. Freddy Fox was too sly to mention the magical Wishing Pebble, for he did not care to have Bertram Bear know that he knew Bertram had it, so he said, "I have found something I wish to show you,

Bertram Bear. Come down to my house and see it!" So Bertram Bear thought to himself, "Freddy Fox does not know that I have a wonderful Wishing Pebble and I will look at his find, then I shall wish for it to be in my house after I see if it is any good! My! Won't Freddy Fox be surprised when he discovers it has disappeared?" And Bertram Bear chuckled to himself to think how he would fool Freddy Fox.

And while Bertram Bear was thinking how he would fool Freddy Fox, Freddy Fox was thinking of how he intended fooling Bertram Bear.

The Raggedys had told Freddy Fox that the magical Wishing Pebble was very white, so Freddy Fox had picked up a white pebble just the size of the real Wishing Pebble, and he thought he could easily exchange it for Bertram Bear's wishing Pebble when Bertram wasn't watching.

And so, Freddy Fox and Bertram Bear walked along through the woods toward the home of Freddy Fox.

By this time Minkie had decided he would run up to Bertram Bear's house and tell Bertram Bear's nice mama how Bertram had taken the Wishing Pebble, so Minkie walked up the path, just a moment or so after Bertram Bear and Freddy Fox had walked down the path.

And Minkie had gone but a short distance when lying right in the center of the path, he saw a white pebble. "Can this be the magical Wishing Pebble?" Minkie wondered. "I will just make a wish and see if it really is!" So he held the pebble in his right hand and closed his eyes and wished. "I wish that I was with Raggedy Ann and Raggedy Andy!" he whispered to himself. Then he opened his eyes, and was so surprised to find himself standing right in front of Raggedy Ann and Raggedy Andy.

"Why, Mister Minkie! Where did you come from?" Raggedy Ann asked and she told Minkie how Bertram Bear had treated Raggedy Andy and herself.

"Do you think Bertram Bear could have lost the real for sure magical Wishing Pebble, Raggedy Ann?" Minkie asked.

"There may be more than one Wishing Pebble!" Raggedy Ann replied.

"We could wish to find out whether Bertram Bear lost it!" Raggedy Andy suggested.

So Minkie wished that he and Raggedy Ann and Raggedy Andy would know just how Bertram might have lost the wonderful Wishing Pebble, and as soon as Minkie made the wish, the three friends laughed, for they saw right away that the Wishing Pebble had dropped through a little hole in Bertram Bear's pocket.

"And now it is yours again, Minkie!" Raggedy Ann said.

"Oh no!" Minkie replied, "The Wishing Pebble is really yours, Raggedy Ann, and I am so glad that I can return it to you. I am so sorry that I was so stingy when I had it before. So you take it and make a lot of nice lovely wishes with it!" And Minkie handed the magical Wishing Pebble to Raggedy Ann.

"Thank you, Mister Minkie," Raggedy Ann said, "I know that now you will find a lot more happiness in the deep, deep woods, because you have changed from a mean little fellow into a nice little fellow!" So she and Raggedy Andy shook hands with Minkie and watched him as he walked sadly away.

But there was a twinkle in Raggedy Ann's shoe-button eyes and she said to Raggedy Andy, "I 'spect Mister Minkie will be shouting with joy when he walks into his home!"

"What makes you 'spect that, Raggedy Ann?" Raggedy Andy wished to know.

"'Cause!" Raggedy Ann replied, "I have already wished that there will be a nice ice cream soda-water fountain in Minkie's living room and right at the side of his kitchen porch that there would be a nice lollypop garden. So now, Minkie can find out just how much fun it will be having his friend help him enjoy the nice things he has!"

And after the two friends had walked along in silence for a few minutes Raggedy Ann laughed and said, "There! You see. Raggedy Andy!"

"See what?" Raggedy Andy asked in surprise.

"Why!" Raggedy Ann chuckled, "I just wished that I would know what you were wishing, and when I found out that you were wishing the Muskrats would also have a lolly-pop garden and another ice cream soda-water fountain I wished for it with the Wishing Pebble, and I'll bet by this time the Muskrats are all calling in their friends to share in their pleasures!"

"Then let's run down and see if the wishes came true, Raggedy Ann!" Raggedy Andy cried, as he caught Raggedy Ann's hand and ran with her down the path through the woods.

CHAPTER TWENTY

AT THE Muskrat home by the side of the Looking-glass Brook there were sounds of merriment. Squeals of delight and happy chattering and laughter.

Mister Muskrat was out upon the bank of the Looking -glass Brook, calling through a horn made of birch-bark: "Everyone is invited to the Muskrat home—we are having a grand party! Hurry and come!" And when the little Meadow-creatures and the Wood-folk heard the cheery invitation, they flew and ran and wiggled towards the Muskrat home.

And, when Mister Muskrat went around to his kitchen porch, he saw that the lolly-pop garden was in the back yard

and there upon small sticks, growing like thousands of colored dandelions, were lovely, candy lolly-pops. So he called to Freddy Fieldmouse and Herbert Hedgehog and some of the other Meadow-folk and had them help him pick enough lolly-pops for each and every guest.

Along the bank of the Looking-glass Brook came Raggady Ann and Raggedy Andy their little cloth faces wreathed in smiles, happy in their knowledge that through their wishes, they had brought pleasure to so many kindly little creatures. "Hurrah for Raggedy Ann with the candy heart!" Everyone cried. "Hurrah for Raggedy Andy, too!" Everyone cried, as they all ran to meet the Raggedys and crowded about to hear how they had recovered the magical Wishing Pebble.

So Raggedy Ann and Raggedy Andy sat down upon the soft yellow grass beside the Looking-glass Brook and with the happy little creatures of the great meadow and the deep, deep woods about them, they related all the difficulties and adventures through which they had passed.

Then, when old Mister Sun had slipped down out of sight and the blue of the evening had settled, changing the purple shadows of the deep, deep woods into a mysterious blackness, the little fire-flies came flitting up from the tall grasses and lighted the way for the Wood-folk and the little Meadow-creatures to reach their homes.

And the brilliant stars and the face of the crescent moon were reflected in the Looking-glass Brook. Raggedy Ann, seeing this, laughed and said, "Isn't the reflection of the moon and stars in the surface of the Looking-glass Brook just like the reflection of happiness we may send out? When someone gives us a moment of happiness, that happiness makes our hearts sing with joyousness and we reflect that happiness from our sunny hearts to some one else, and so in turn it is reflected to others, on and on!"

Then the Raggedys and Mr. and Mrs. Muskrat went into the Muskrat home and in ten minutes, all were sound asleep in their little soft beds, dreaming the dreams which are always brought to heads filled with happy thoughts.

CHAPTER TWENTY-ONE

BRIGHT and early in the morning, in fact the smiling face of the great Mister Sun had just peeped over the trees in the deep, deep woods, again painting the great meadow in its morning bath of golden light, Mrs. Muskrat hopped out of bed and slipped quietly to the kitchen intending to make no noise and awaken the Raggedys.

Mrs. Muskrat knew how to make the loveliest pancakes, all a golden brown on both sides. She wanted to make a lot before she called Mr. Muskrat and Raggedy Ann and Raggedy Andy.

But when Mrs. Muskrat opened the kitchen door she gave a squeal of surprise for there, sitting upon a chair by the kitchen door, his face washed nice and clean and his shoe-button eyes with all the sleep dust wiped from them, sat Raggedy Andy.

There beside the kitchen table, her sleeves rolled up and wearing a large apron, was Raggedy Ann.

"Now you just sit down beside Raggedy Andy!" Mrs. Muskrat laughed. "I got up early so that I could make the pancakes. Then when I had a lot baked I meant to call you both."

Presently Mr. Muskrat came from his bed-room and as soon as he had washed his face breakfast was ready.

"What did you do with the Wishing Pebble, Raggedy Ann?" Mr. Muskrat asked after all had eaten sixteen pancakes with maple syrup on them. "Did you push it down in the sand again?" and he and all the rest laughed at the recollection of how they had searched for the lost pebble.

"Indeed! I didn't, Mr. Muskrat!" Raggedy Ann replied as she wiped the syrup from around Raggedy Andy's mouth with her napkin, "I have it wrapped up carefully in my pocket hanky and here it is!" She took her hanky with the blue border from her pocket and showed Mr. and Mrs. Muskrat the wonderful Wishing Pebble and the light of the morning sun shone into the white of the Wishing Pebble and seemed to wink cheerily.

"Isn't it white and smooth and round?" Mrs. Muskrat said, "No wonder it is so magical! But Raggedy Ann, you should not carry such a magical thing in a pocket hanky! What if you should lose it?"

"I don't know what else to do with it!" Raggedy Ann replied. "If I just put it in my apron pocket, and that's the only pocket I have, I would be sure to lose it—but if I keep it wrapped in my pocket hanky and lose the hanky, it will be much easier to find!"

"I know!" Mrs. Muskrat cried as she ran into her bed room and came out with a sewing basket, "I will snip a little hole in Raggedy Ann's body and—"

"Oh dear no!" Mr. Muskrat cried, jumping up when Mrs. Muskrat took out a pair of scissors. "You mustn't hurt Raggedy Ann!"

"Silly!" Mrs. Muskrat laughed, as she gave Mr. Muskrat a playful pinch on his nose. "Don't you know Raggedy Ann and Raggedy Andy are made of cloth and stuffed with nice clean white cotton? It doesn't hurt them to be snipped open with a pair of scissors. Then when I have made a tiny slit in Raggedy Ann's cloth body, I will poke the magical Wishing Pebble way into the soft cotton stuffing and sew the hole up. Then she cannot ever lose the Wishing Pebble unless she gets lost herself!"

So Mrs. Muskrat took off Raggedy Ann's apron and dress and snipped a tiny hole in Raggedy Ann's cloth back. Then she poked the Wishing Pebble way into the cotton stuffing and in a few moments had the hole sewed up.

Raggedy Ann kissed Mrs. Muskrat and thanked her. "Is there any other nice thing I could wish for you, Mrs. Muskrat?" Raggedy Ann asked.

"Dear me, no, Raggedy Ann!" Mrs. Muskrat replied. "We have the lovely ice cream soda-water fountain in our living room and the lolly-pop garden at the kitchen door. What more could we wish for to make our friends any happier?"

"Then I 'spect our adventure is at an end!" Raggedy Ann said. "For Raggedy Andy and I must return to the nursery and we have a long way to go!"

The kindly Muskrats did not like to see Raggedy Ann and Raggedy Andy leave, but they also knew they must not be selfish with their friends, so they gave Raggedy Ann and Raggedy Andy a lot of tight hugs, then watched the two dolls as they walked away through the tall yellow grass.

"What a pleasure it is to have generous, kindly friends who love us!" Mrs. Muskrat said, as she wiped her eyes with the corner of her apron.

And, as Raggedy Ann and Raggedy Andy with an arm about each other walked towards their home, the same pleasant thoughts ran through their little cotton-stuffed heads, and while they said never a word to each other, each knew and felt the other shared the same joyousness.

And, as you surely must know, there is no feeling which brings as much true sunshine to our hearts as the happiness of honest, loving friendship.

RAGGEDY ANN AND THE PAPER DRAGON

RAGGEDY ANN AND THE PAPER DRAGON

Written and Illustrated by

JOHNNY GRUELLE

To

EVELYN, DAVID

and

JUDY CHAMBERS

With the wish that their pathway
through life may be bordered with
the flowers of friendship.

JOHNNY GRUELLE
Norwalk, Connecticut
September 2, 1925

CHAPTER ONE

RAGGEDY Ann and Raggedy Andy were two rag dolls. They were stuffed with nice clean white cotton and their faces were painted on them. Both Raggedy Ann and Raggedy Andy wore very cheery smiles and were friendly, happy little creatures.

The two Raggedys lived in the nursery at Marcella's house and always had great fun with the other dolls, for as you surely must know, dolls play together when there are no real for sure people around to watch them. And although Raggedy Ann and Raggedy Andy loved all the other dolls in the nursery very much, still at times they liked to leave the nursery and walk down through the deep, deep woods filled with fairies 'n everything, because there they found strange adventures.

Once before, in adventuring in the deep, deep woods Raggedy Ann and Raggedy Andy had found a very magical stick. It was a wishing stick and made every wish come true. This stick had been sewed inside Raggedy Andy's cotton stuffed body and just looking at him, no one would guess he could make wishes come true.

Raggedy Ann had been as fortunate as Raggedy Andy, for on one adventure in the deep, deep woods, Raggedy Ann had found a very Magical Wishing Pebble, and this was sewed up inside her cotton stuffed body, so that Raggedy

Ann, like Raggedy Andy, could make her wishes come true too. So, this day, when the two Raggedys kissed the other dolls in the nursery good-bye and skipped out through the garden gate and down the path leading to the deep, deep woods, their little cotton stuffed bodies tingled with excitement, for they both felt they were running to meet some wonderful adventures. And indeed, this was true. The Raggedys had gone but a short distance into the deep, deep woods when Raggedy Andy heard something.

"Didn't that sound like some one calling for help?" Raggedy Andy asked as he caught Raggedy Ann's arm.

"I heard something, but I could not hear just what was said," Raggedy Ann replied in a whisper.

"Listen," Raggedy Andy said. "There it is again!"

"HELP! HELP!" some one cried.

"It's over the other side of that great big stone," Raggedy Ann whispered. "Let's run over real easy and climb on the stone, then we can see who it is."

The two Raggedys caught hold of hands and ran over to the large stone and when they reached it they saw little steps leading to the top. Up the steps they climbed until they could look over the top of the great stone.

"I've got you this time," a voice said. "And this time I will not let you get away."

"Oh, please Mister Doodle, don't take me to your house and make me chop the wood for you! I have to run to the store to get a penny's worth of needle eyes for mama and hurry right back so she can finish her sewing. Then I have to—"

"HA! You won't run to the store today," Mister Doodle laughed. "I've got a lot of wood to be chopped and I am too tired to do it myself so you got to do it!"

"You are a mean man, Mister Doodle, and I just bet you had better run along home and chop the wood yourself before you get in trouble," Raggedy Ann said from the top of the stone.

"Is that so?" Mister Doodle laughed "I guess I will take Marggy home to chop my wood if I want to." And Mister Doodle started to pull the little girl along behind him through the woods.

"Now I'll tell you what, Mister Doodle," cried Raggedy Ann. "If you do not let go of Marggy before I count three, you'll find yourself standing on your head."

"Ha! Ha! Ha!" Mister Doodle laughed, for you see, he did not know that all Raggedy Ann or Andy had to do was to make a wish and the wish would come true, "I'd like to see a rag doll keep me from taking Marggy home to chop the wood for me!"

"ONE," said Raggedy Ann, "two", she added after a pause, "now you better let go," she warned. But Mister Doodle gave Marggy a pull and started away.

"Alright," said Raggedy Ann. "THREE!"

"And I wish that he bumps up and down real hard," said Raggedy Andy as Mister Doodle turned upside down and stood upon his head.

"Oh! You must be fairies!" Marggy cried as she saw Mister Doodle do just as the two Raggedys had wished.

"No, we are only two rag dolls, Marggy," Raggedy Ann said as she and Andy jumped from the large stone. "Now let's run to your house before Mister Doodle gets upon his feet again!" And catching Marggy's hands, the two Raggedys ran through the woods until they came to a little house with an open door.

"Ha!" said someone over by the fireplace.

"Is that your mother, Marggy?" Raggedy Ann asked as she saw a woman in an easy chair watching a pot hanging over cold ashes.

"Dear me, no!" Marggy replied. "I tried to tell you this was Mister Doodle's house, but you ran so fast I could not catch my breath."

"Then is that Missus Doodle?" Raggedy Andy asked.

"Yes, I am," Missus Doodle said. "And you are just in time too. I want to get supper and the food won't cook, because I have no fire. One of you carry some wood in from the other room and light it. Mister Doodle will be here in a minute."

Marggy started to get the wood for Missus Doodle, but Raggedy Andy stopped her. "How long have you been sitting here watching that pot, Mrs. Doodle?"

"Ever since early this morning," Mrs. Doodle replied. "But what has that to do with getting the wood?"

"It hasn't anything to do with it," Raggedy Andy replied. "Except that we will not get the wood for you when you try to make us do it. If you had asked one of us real nice, we would have been pleased to get the wood and start the fire."

"Then into the cage you go!" cried Mrs. Doodle as she jumped out of her chair and caught Raggedy Andy.

"Here!" Marggy cried as she caught Mrs. Doodle's arm. "You put Raggedy Andy down right away!"

Mrs. Doodle walked out into the other room and stuffed Raggedy Andy into an empty parrot cage hanging on the wall. Then she ran after Raggedy Ann and when she caught her, she stuffed Raggedy Ann in beside Raggedy Andy.

"Polly wants a cracker!" Raggedy Andy cried just like a parrot.

"Now!" Mrs. Doodle cried as she gave Marggy's ear a twist, "get busy and build the fire!" And she pushed the little girl into the wood room.

"Bang! Bang! Bang!" someone knocked on the front door.

"Who is it?" asked Mrs. Doodle as she walked to the door.

"It's me, Mr. Doodle! Just wait until I catch Raggedy Ann and Raggedy Andy and Marggy!"

"Ha! Ha! Ha!" Mrs. Doodle laughed. "Then come right in for the two Raggedys are in the parrot cage!"

"Ha," Mr. Doodle said as he picked up a stick. "Show me where they are."

"Polly wants a cracker!" Raggedy Andy cried from the parrot cage just like a parrot.

"Maybe you should not tease him, Raggedy Andy," Raggedy Ann said.

Raggedy Andy just laughed when Mr. Doodle walked in the room. "You just watch, Raggedy Ann," he whispered. Then he cried to Mr. Doodle, "Hello Mr. Doodle, how did it feel to dance around on your head?"

Mr. Doodle was very, very angry. "I'll show you now that you are fastened up in the parrot cage! I'll hit the cage with this big stick and knock it off the nail, then the cage will fall on the floor and you will both bump your heads!"

Mr. Doodle threw the big stick right at the cage, but Raggedy Andy, who had a wishing stick sewed inside his rag body made a wish the moment Mr. Doodle came in the house. So when Mr. Doodle threw the stick, instead of the stick knocking the parrot cage from the nail, the stick circled around the parrot cage and came flying back at Mr. Doodle's head.

"Wow!" Mr. Doodle cried as the stick knocked his hat off his head. "What made that stick bounce that way?"

"You didn't hit the parrot cage, that's why," said Mrs. Doodle.

Mr. Doodle picked up the stick and took careful aim. "This time I'll knock the cage down and bump the Raggedys' heads, I'll bet a nickel!"

And he threw the stick so hard that when it circled around the parrot cage again, it sailed right back and cracked Mr. Doodle on top of his head. This made Mr. Doodle sit down on the floor so hard he jarred a vase off the mantel piece.

"Now see what you did!" Mrs. Doodle cried as she hit Mr. Doodle with the broom. "You broke my nicest vase! I'll hit the cage this time and bump the Raggedys' heads." Then Mrs. Doodle threw the broom at the parrot cage, but the broom circled around the edge just as the stick had done and after striking Mrs. Doodle and knocking her down, it flew along the wall and knocked down three pictures.

Raggedy Ann and Raggedy Andy in the parrot cage had to hold their rag sides to keep from laughing, for the harder Mr. and Mrs. Doodle tried to knock down the parrot cage, the more damage they did until finally their whole house was covered with broken vases and pictures and broken dishes and both of them had a lot of bumps on the top of their heads.

"You see," Raggedy Andy said from the parrot cage. "Whenever you try to injure another, you always harm yourselves. Let this be a lesson to you!"

Now this made Raggedy Ann and Raggedy Andy feel sorry, for although the Doodles had tried to injure the Raggedys, still the Raggedys did not wish to injure the Doodles in return. So Raggedy Andy made a wish that all the broken things would be mended right away. And soon everything was just as good as new.

Then when Mr. and Mrs. Doodle saw everything was not broken, they could not understand what had happened, for you see, they did not know that every time the Raggedys made a wish, the wish came true.

"I guess we must have been dreaming," Mr. Doodle said as he got up from the floor.

"I guess we were," Mrs. Doodle said.

"No, you were not dreaming," Raggedy Andy said. "You will find that every time you try to injure another, you will hurt yourself twice as much."

Now Mr. and Mrs. Doodle did not believe this was true, so they said, "The Raggedys must have a magic charm in their pockets, for every time they make a wish, the wish comes true. So we must take the magic charms away from them, and then we can make all our wishes come true."

"The first thing I shall wish for will be a big piano, then I will sit and play pretty music all day long," said Mrs. Doodle.

"Indeed!" Mr. Doodle replied. "I shall have the first wish. I shall wish for an automobile!"

Then the Doodles stamped their feet and pulled each other's noses. While they were quarreling, Raggedy Ann and Raggedy Andy jumped out of the parrot cage, opened the door real easy and slipped outside.

"Oh dear," Raggedy Ann said as she stopped running, "We ran away from the Doodles' house and left Marggy there! Now the Doodles will be so angry when they find we have escaped, they will make Marggy chop all their wood and build their fires and do their cooking!"

"Then we must hurry right back and take Marggy away from Mr. Doodle's house," said Raggedy Andy as he turned back.

When the Raggedys came to Mr. and Mrs. Doodle's house they could hear a lot of noise inside so they walked right in without knocking.

"You must let me run home to my Mama," Marggy said to Mr. Doodle.

"Not until you chop up all the wood for us and make the fire and do the cooking," Mr. Doodle said. "Mrs. Doodle and I are too tired to do it." Then Mr. Doodle caught hold of the little girl's arm and pulled her to the wood pile. "There now," he said as he shut the door. "Don't come out until the wood is all chopped."

Marggy sat down in a corner of the wood room and began crying, for she was too small to chop wood. But Raggedy Ann and Raggedy Andy had slipped into the room when Mr. Doodle wasn't looking, so they wiped Marggy's tears away and said, "Don't cry, Marggy, we will rescue you some way."

"But Mr. Doodle has locked the door tight," said Marggy. "And we can't get out!"

Raggedy Ann peeped through the key hole and saw Mr. and Mrs. Doodle sitting in easy chairs. "We will rest while Marggy chops the wood," said Mrs. Doodle.

"Ha! Ha!" Raggedy Ann thought to herself. 'If you are that lazy, it will just serve you right if we can fool you." And she thought and thought until she ripped two stitches in the top of her rag head, then she made a wish. It was a queer wish. Raggedy Ann wished that she and Raggedy Andy and Marggy were only as large as tiny little weeny weeny bugs. And just as soon as the wish came true, the three of them walked right out through the crack under the back door. Next Raggedy Ann made a wish that they would become large again. Then they caught hold of hands and ran for Marggy's house as fast as they could go.

"The joke I played on Mr. and Mrs. Doodle was a good one," Raggedy Ann laughed. "After we escaped from the Doodles' house, I wished that all the wood would grow larger! Now when Mr. Doodle finds he has to chop it after all, he will have more work to do!"

"And that will serve him just right too," Raggedy Andy laughed. "For whenever anyone puts off doing a thing, hoping that someone else will come along and do it for him, he always finds that the work seems harder."

"You should tell your Daddy to speak to Mr. Doodle," said Raggedy Ann to Marggy.

"Oh, dear me," Marggy replied. "I haven't any Daddy. He went out in the woods a long time ago and never came back."

"Well, well, well," the Raggedys both said. "Then we must search for him and maybe we can find him and bring him home to you and your Mama."

CHAPTER TWO

WHEN Marggy told her Mama that the Raggedys were going to search for her Daddy she was very happy.

"I tell you what let's do," said Raggedy Ann. "Let's take a ball of your Mama's darning cotton and make a wish that the cotton will roll in front of us until it comes to where your Daddy is."

Even Marggy's Mama thought this would be lots of fun, so she got a ball of red cotton and Raggedy Ann made the wish. "Now we will follow the pretty red ball until it rolls to your Daddy," said Raggedy Ann.

"I believe we had better take some cream puffs and doughnuts with us," Marggy's Mama said. "For we may get hungry." So she filled a basket with doughnuts and cream puffs, then they all followed the red ball as it rolled through the woods.

After the red ball had rolled along for almost a mile our friends came to a little house beside the path and just as the red ball came to the front door, a funny little old woman ran out and caught it.

"Oh my!" Raggedy Ann said. "You mustn't pick up the little red ball! We are following it!"

Then the funny little old woman made a face at Raggedy

Ann. "I found it!" she cried. "I need some red cotton to mend my red stockings!"

"Oh dear! What shall we do?" Marggy's Mama asked.

"There isn't anything you can do!" the funny little old woman replied. "The red cotton is mine now!" And with this, she started into the house with the little red ball.

Now maybe you don't know it, but when Raggedy Ann made the wish for the red ball to roll in front of them, this made the little red ball a magical ball, so when the funny little old woman tried to take the ball into her house, the magic ball pulled just as hard in the opposite direction.

My! How the funny little old woman tussled. She pulled and the ball pulled until finally the ball pulled the hardest and it pulled the funny little old woman right down the path in front of our friends.

"If you do not let go of the little red ball, you will wear all the soles off your shoes," Raggedy Ann said.

"I will never, never let go!" cried the funny little old woman.

The funny little old woman was very determined and she held on to the little red ball, even when it pulled her along and made her feet slide over the gravel. "You will wear out your nice shoes," Marggy's Mama said.

"I don't care!" cried the funny little old woman. "You will have to buy me new ones!"

"Did you ever hear the like!" Raggedy Andy exclaimed. "Here the funny little old woman tries to take our magical ball and when she can't take it, she blames us if she wears out her shoes scuffing along!"

The funny little old woman held her feet out in front of her and just slid along the path, and this held the little red ball back just enough so that Raggedy Ann and Raggedy Andy and Marggy and her Mama had to walk real slow or else step upon the funny little old woman's heels.

"I guess we'll have to help the little red ball," Raggedy Andy said. "It has a hard time pulling the funny little old woman along. I'll help the ball by pushing the funny little old woman."

But when Raggedy Andy helped the little red ball by pushing on the funny little old woman, she slid over the gravel in the path so fast, it made her feet burn, so she sat right down plunk in the path and wouldn't budge a speck.

"Now what shall we do?" Raggedy Andy asked as he scratched his head.

"I shan't budge!" the funny little old woman cried. "This little red ball is mine and I shall take it home!"

"I feel like boxing her ears," Marggy's Mama cried. "The funny little old woman is just like a spoilt child, and it would teach her a lesson if some one paddywhacked her."

"Maybe after she rests awhile she will stand up again," said Raggedy Andy. "Then the little red ball will pull her along."

So while they waited for the funny little old woman to stand up, Marggy's Mama got out the cream puffs and doughnuts.

"We'll give you a doughnut, if you'd like one," Raggedy Ann said to the funny little old woman. But the funny little old woman just shook her head and held tightly to the little red ball.

"I shall hang on to the little red magic ball until I can take it home with me," the funny little old woman said. "I need some red yarn to darn my stockings with."

"But if you do not let go of the little red magic ball, you will wear the soles off your shoes scuffing along," said Raggedy Andy. "Then you'll have to go to the shoe maker and have new soles put on your shoes."

"Maybe when we come to a brook, the little red ball will pull the funny little old woman right into the water," Marggy said.

But even when they came to a little brook, the funny little old woman held to the little red magic ball. It pulled her right through the water so she was wet up to her knees.

"Dear me," Raggedy Ann said. "We will never find Marggy's Daddy if the funny little old woman keeps holding the magic ball back all the time! We would have been miles farther if the ball had been allowed to roll along as fast as it started."

"Maybe if I carried the funny little old woman she wouldn't pull back on the magic ball all the time," said Raggedy Andy.

So Raggedy Andy picked up the funny little old woman and started to carry her the way the little red magic ball wanted to go, but she kicked and twisted and wiggled and scolded so hard, she knocked Raggedy Andy right over backwards. And when Raggedy Andy fell down, the funny little old woman bumped her head on a stone so hard, she forgot all about holding the little red magic ball and held her head instead.

"It was all your fault!" she cried to Raggedy Andy. "If you had not tried to carry me, I would not have bumped my head!"

"I'm sorry," Raggedy Andy said, for he would not have had the funny little old woman bump her head on purpose. "But now you have let go of our little red magic ball and we can follow it and find Marggy's Daddy, I will give you a nice big ball of red cotton."

The funny little old woman was so pleased she dried her tears and ran right home.

CHAPTER THREE

RAGGEDY ANN and Raggedy Andy and Marggy and her Mama followed the little red magical ball of darning cotton through the woods until they came to a gate made of logs. The little red magical ball rolled through the gate and our friends started to follow it, when a great big Dragon, just like the Dragons you see in Chinese pictures, came right out and opened its mouth and the little red magical ball of darning cotton rolled inside.

"Oh, dear!" cried Marggy's Mama as she sat down on a stone and wiped her eyes with her apron. "Now the little red magical ball is gone and we will never find Daddy."

"Why did you swallow our little red magical ball of darning cotton?" Raggedy Ann asked the great big dragon.

"Because," the Dragon replied.

"That isn't any reason at all," Raggedy Ann said. "And you ought to be ashamed of yourself! That's what!"

"Well, I'm not," the great big large Dragon replied as it wiggled its long tail. And when Raggedy Ann pointed her rag hand at its nose to make it feel ashamed of itself, the great big large Dragon opened its great large mouth real wide and went, "Gobble! Gobble!"

"Here! You stop that, Mister Dragon!" Raggedy Andy cried, but he was too late for the great big large Dragon had swallowed Raggedy Ann completely.

"Now then, you've gone and done it!" Raggedy Andy cried as he hunted around for a great big stick.

"What are you going to do with that great big stick?" the Dragon asked as he twirled his long tail.

"You just wait and see! That's what!" Raggedy Andy said as he rolled up his sleeves.

"Are we going to have a fight?" the Dragon asked.

Raggedy Andy did not answer the Dragon. Instead, he walked right up to it holding the large stick in front of him. When Raggedy Andy came up to him, the Dragon opened his great big mouth and started to say "Gobble!" Gobble!" just like he had done when he swallowed Raggedy Ann, but Raggedy Andy was too smart for him. Raggedy Andy just as quick as a wink, put the large stick in the Dragon's mouth and this held the Dragon's mouth wide open.

My! How the Dragon wiggled and wobbled his long tail, but it did no good, for he could not get the stick out of his mouth. And when he wiggled and wobbled his long tail Raggedy Andy and Marggy and her Mama could hear Raggedy Ann and the little red magical ball rattling around way back inside the Dragon. Then they heard a funny scratching sound and here came Raggedy Ann crawling out.

"The Dragon is just made out of paper and thin slats of wood!" Raggedy Ann laughed.

"The reason I did not fight the great big large Dragon was because I saw right away that he was made out of paper," said Raggedy Andy. "And if I had hit him upon the head with the large stick, I would have broken his head in pieces."

"Are you going to take the stick out of his mouth?" Marggy's Mama asked Raggedy Andy, "The great big Dragon might eat someone else up just as he did Raggedy Ann."

Raggedy Ann laughed. "The great big Dragon wouldn't harm anyone even if he did swallow them," she said. "For he is hollow all the way to the tip of his tail. And if he swallowed anyone, all they would have to do would be to kick real hard and they could kick a large hole right through him."

Raggedy Andy walked up to the large paper Dragon and took the big stick out of its mouth. "There," said Raggedy Andy. "Does that feel better?"

"Yes indeed!" the Dragon replied. "When my mouth was propped open with the stick, it made cold chills run all the way to the tip end of my long tail, and it felt just like someone had left the front door wide open on a cold day."

"Then after this, you mustn't swallow anyone again," said Raggedy Andy.

"I did not swallow Raggedy Ann," the Dragon replied.

"No, he didn't, that's true," Raggedy Ann agreed. "I jumped into his mouth, because I saw right away he was made out of paper and thin slats of wood. I knew someone had to rescue the little red magical ball of darning cotton or we would never find Marggy's Daddy."

"What do you eat, Mister Dragon?" Marggy's Mama asked as she walked up and thumped the Dragon's head to see if he really and truly was paper.

"I never eat anything," the Dragon replied, "But lots of times when I yawn the wind blows pieces of paper right in my mouth and dry leaves and I do not know how to get them out again! I'm afraid maybe if mice find out I have pieces of paper and nice dry leaves in me, they might build nests in my paper body. And you know how mice are, sometimes they chew holes in things."

"I tell you what let's do! Let's pull him up into a tree by the tip end of his tail and shake all the leaves and pieces of paper out," Raggedy Andy said.

Marggy and her Mama couldn't climb trees like Raggedy Ann and Raggedy Andy, so they stayed upon the ground and boosted the paper Dragon's tail up to Raggedy Ann and Andy. Then Raggedy Ann and Raggedy Andy shook the paper Dragon's tail until all the leaves and pieces of paper rattled down to his mouth. Then Marggy and her Mama cleaned all the leaves and paper out of the paper Dragon's mouth and he felt very, very much better.

Then Raggedy Ann and Raggedy Andy and Marggy and her Mama told the paper Dragon good-bye and followed the little red magical ball of darning cotton through the woods.

CHAPTER FOUR

RAGGEDY ANN and Raggedy Andy and Marggy and her Mama had gone only a short way when they heard a loud noise in back of them.

"Land sakes!" cried Raggedy Ann. "What can be making all that racket?" But because the others did not know, of course they could not tell, so they just had to wait until whatever made the racket reached them.

The noise grew louder and louder until they saw the paper Dragon coming through the woods as fast as he could wiggle. The paper Dragon wiggled and twisted along so fast his long tail bumped against the trees blumpity smack, crash, blump!

"Dear me! Something must be wrong with the paper Dragon!" Raggedy Ann said. "He will tear a lot of holes in his sides if he isn't careful the way he smacks into the trees and stones!"

The paper Dragon was so out of breath when he reached Raggedy Ann all he could say was "Run!" And he said it with such a wheeze no one could understand what he said.

"Whatever made you wiggle so fast through the woods, Mister Dragon?" Raggedy Andy asked. "You've snagged a lot of holes in your tail, and while you rest we will mend them with paper and glue."

"But we haven't any glue!" Marggy's Mama said.

"Maybe we can use the cream out of a cream puff!" Raggedy Ann suggested. And as there were lots of pieces of paper blowing about through the woods Raggedy Ann and Raggedy Andy soon stuck patches on every hole in the paper Dragon's body.

"Ah! That feels ever so much better," the paper Dragon said. "I guess the reason I got out of breath was because I had so many holes in my long body, and the air leaked out of the holes."

"Maybe you ran with your mouth open," Marggy said.

"Yes, that's true," the Dragon replied. "Let's see now, what was I going to tell you? I guess it slipped out of the holes, for I have completely forgotten what it was."

"Try to think real hard," suggested Raggedy Andy. "Raggedy Ann and I often think so hard we rip stitches out of our heads."

"But I have no stitches in my head," the Dragon replied.

"Then we'll just sit here and wait until you think without ripping any stitches," said Raggedy Ann.

So the Raggedys and Marggy and her Mama sat down and waited for the Dragon to remember.

"Can't you remember what it was?" Raggedy Andy asked after they had sat there awhile.

"I haven't the least idea," the paper Dragon replied. "I can't seem to think very well."

"Maybe if you would scratch your head, it would help," said Raggedy Ann.

"Oh, he can't scratch his head," Raggedy Andy laughed. "He hasn't any hands to scratch with."

"Of course not," Raggedy Ann laughed. "It was silly of me to suggest it!"

"But we could take sticks and scratch his head for him," Marggy said.

"Maybe that will help," the paper Dragon said.

So Raggedy Ann and Raggedy Andy and Marggy and her Mama each got a stick and scratched the Dragon's head.

JOHNNY GRUELLE

After they had scratched awhile, the paper Dragon said, "That's enough! I remember what it was now! You must run and run fast!"

"But why should we run?" Raggedy Ann asked. "If we run, we will get ahead of the little magical red ball of darning cotton and you know, the little red ball rolls through the woods and is leading us to where Marggy's Daddy is."

"Well, you had better run anyway!" the Dragon said. "For there's a queer man running after you, and the only reason he isn't here now is because I wiggled through the woods so much faster than he can run."

"Who is it?" Raggedy Ann asked of the others.

"I'll tell you who it is," the Dragon said. "It's Mr. Doodle!"

"Oh dear!" Marggy cried. "He wants to take me back to his house to chop wood for him!"

"Well, he will never do that," Raggedy Andy said. "We will hide some place and wait until he runs by, then we will go another way."

"Here's a dandy place to hide," said Raggedy Ann. "Quick! Everyone get in this great big hollow tree. Afterwards we will catch up with the magic ball."

So they all squeezed into the great big hollow tree. Even the Dragon, and waited for Mr. Doodle to run by them.

"Here he comes now, I can hear him!" the Dragon said to Raggedy Ann and Raggedy Andy and Marggy and her Mama. The Dragon was the last to crawl into the great big hollow tree so he could hear better than the others.

"He's coming lickety split through the woods," the Dragon whispered.

"Goody! Now he's going by! It's stuffy in here all crowded together and I will be glad when Mr. Doodle runs past," said Raggedy Ann.

"Oh shucks!" the Dragon cried out loud.

"Be quiet!" Raggedy Ann said. "He will hear you sure!"

"That's just it!" the Dragon said. "He has heard us and he is pulling and yanking my tail now!"

"He's pulling me out of the tree!" the Dragon wailed.

Indeed, this was true, for the others soon felt the Dragon slipping and slipping until suddenly he was yanked right out of the great big hollow tree.

"Ha! Ha! Ha!" laughed Mr. Doddle. "You thought you could fool me did you?"

"How did you know where we were?" Raggedy Andy asked as he and the others came out.

"Why, who wouldn't know where you were when the foolish Dragon had ten or fifteen feet of his tail sticking out of the tree!"

"I knew I would spoil it all, if I hid in the tree with you! I'm so sorry!" the Dragon cried.

"Don't you care," Raggedy Andy whispered. "You did the best you knew how and we are glad of that."

"Now," said Mr. Doodle. "I've come to take Marggy home with me to chop the wood."

"Dear me," Raggedy Ann exclaimed. "If you worked as hard chopping your wood as you have chasing us, you would have the wood all chopped!"

"I'm too tired to chop wood, I tell you," Mr. Doodle shouted as he gave Marggy's arm a pull.

"Now see here," the Dragon cried. "I guess we will have to fight!" So Mr. Doodle took off his coat and rolled up his sleeves. "The rest of you had better keep back out of the way," he said.

So Raggedy Ann passed the doughnuts and cream puffs. "For," she said as they took seats back out of the way. "We might as well have lunch while we wait for the Dragon to fight Mr. Doodle."

The fight between Mr. Doodle and the Dragon was a great sight to see. The Dragon could growl very loud when he wanted to and he growled louder than usual. But Mr. Doodle, even if he was so lazy that he wanted Marggy to chop his wood

for him, was very brave and every time the Dragon growled, Mr. Doodle stuck out his tongue at the Dragon.

This made the Dragon growl louder than ever and Raggedy Andy grew so excited he put a cream puff into his eye instead of his mouth and the cream puff covered his shoe button eye so that he could only watch the fight with one eye until Raggedy Ann wiped the cream puff off with her pocket hanky. The little white one with blue flowers on it.

Each time the Dragon rushed at Mr. Doodle and growled, Mr. Doodle jumped back. And each time Mr. Doodle rushed at the Dragon, the Dragon jumped back. And the fight lasted until both Mr. Doodle and the Dragon grew so excited, they forgot what they were doing, and both rushed at each other at the same time. This surprised the Dragon so much, he stopped suddenly and opened his mouth and he had no sooner done this than Mr. Doodle, who was as much surprised as the Dragon, lost his balance and fell right into the Dragon's mouth.

"Hm!" the Dragon said. "The great fight is over!"

"I'm glad that you swallowed Mr. Doodle instead of Mr. Doodle swallowing you!" Raggedy Andy told the Dragon as he patted him upon the head.

"Silly!" Raggedy Ann laughed at Raggedy Andy. "How could Mr. Doodle swallow the Dragon when the Dragon is so much larger?"

"I never thought of that," Raggedy Andy giggled. He knew when the joke was on him.

But suddenly the Dragon looked worried and it only took Raggedy Andy a moment to find out why. Mr. Doodle, inside the paper Dragon had started stomping around.

"If you don't let me out, I'll kick out all your slats!" Mr. Doodle shouted from inside the paper Dragon.

"I believe I had better let him out," the Dragon said. "I think he has nails in his shoes!"

So the Dragon opened his mouth and Mr. Doodle walked out. Mr. Doodle was so tired though, he had to sit down and rest. "We'll have another fight just as soon as I rest up a bit."

And because they did not believe in being stingy, Raggedy Ann and Raggedy Andy gave Mr. Doodle three cream puffs and six doughnuts to help him rest.

After resting and eating three cream puffs and six doughnuts, Mr. Doodle jumped to his feet. "Now we must continue our fight!" he cried to the Dragon.

"I won't fight you if you fall inside my mouth again and kick around like you did before. Your shoes have nails in them!" the Dragon said.

"I guess I'll take off my shoes then," Mr. Doodle agreed. "That will make it a fair fight, don't you think?"

When Mr. Doodle had taken off his shoes with the nails in the bottom the Dragon said, "I will never permit you to take Marggy home with you to chop your wood."

And Mr. Doodle replied, "And I will never permit you to not permit me to take Marggy home with me to chop my wood." And with this, Mr. Doodle stuck out his tongue at the Dragon and the Dragon growled very loud at Mr. Doodle. Then Mr. Doodle pushed upon the Dragon and the Dragon pushed upon Mr. Doodle and back and forth they tussled until finally the Dragon pushed the hardest and pushed Mr. Doodle over on his back.

Of course you have guessed by this time that Mr. Doodle was losing the fight with the Dragon, and it made him so angry he lost his temper, and before anyone could say, "Scat!" Mr. Doodle picked up a stone and threw it right smack dab through the kind Dragon's paper side.

"Aren't you ashamed of yourself, Mr. Doodle?" Raggedy Ann cried.

"I don't care," Mr. Doodle replied. "He shouldn't have pushed me over on my back, that's what!"

Marggy's Mama, before she stopped to think that Mr. Doodle did not belong to her, caught Mr. Doodle and turned him over her knee. And I wish that you could have heard the paddywhacks she gave him with her slipper. When Marggy's Mama had finished paddywacking Mr. Doodle, Mr. Doodle ran home as fast as he could.

"Ha! Ha! Ha!" the Dragon laughed in spite of the hole in his side, "Marggy's Mama is the one who really won the great fight!"

Raggedy Andy hunted around through the woods until he found a Sunday newspaper and with this and some of the cream from the cream puffs, Raggedy Andy and Raggedy Ann covered the hole in the paper Dragon's side. The Sunday newspaper was printed in colors and it made the paper Dragon much prettier than he had been and everyone told him so. And after they had thanked the kindly paper Dragon for rescuing Marggy from Mr. Doodle, they left the Dragon trying to wiggle around so that he could see the beautiful Sunday newspaper patch they had pasted on his side.

CHAPTER FIVE

"IT'S nice to go adventuring through the lovely woods!" Raggedy Ann said as they walked along.

"Yes, indeed it is," Marggy's Mama replied. "And wasn't it fortunate we met the kind paper Dragon! If it had not been for him, old Mr. Doodle would have taken Marggy home with him to chop his wood, and then we would not have been able to hunt any further for Marggy's Daddy."

"Dear me suz!" Raggedy Ann exclaimed as she looked back. "Here comes Mr. Doodle! Why doesn't he let us alone!"

"I'll get a nice long switch and we'll see about this!" Marggy's Mama said very severe-like, but when Mr. Doodle came running up, Marggy's Mama did not have to use the switch because Mr. Doodle had a box in his hands and said, "See what I found back in the woods!"

The box was made of shiny wood and on the front were black shiny knobs with little white numbers on them.

"What is it, Mr. Doodle?" Marggy's Mama asked, forgetting that she held the nice long switch.

"I do not know!" Mr. Doodle replied. "After I had the fight with the paper Dragon and after Marggy's Mama paddywhacked me, I ran as fast as I could until I grew very tired; then I sat down to rest, and right in front of me in a hollow tree I saw this lovely box."

"I'll bet a nickel it is a magic box," Raggedy Andy said.

"Let's all sit down and maybe we can think what the box is for," Raggedy Ann suggested. So while they sat and thought, Marggy's Mama gave them each a cream puff, for everyone knows, you can think ever so much better while eating cream puffs.

Finally Raggedy Ann said, "I'll tell you what let's do!"

"What?" Mr. Doodle asked.

"All of you run over and hide in that hollow tree and I will open the box, then if a Magician, or a Genei hops out he won't know where you are."

"No sir!" Raggedy Andy said, very decidedly. "Mr. Doodle found the box and it belongs to him, so if there is a Magician, or a Genei in the magic box then Mr. Doodle can open it so that he will be caught instead of you, Raggedy Ann."

"That is true!" Mr. Doodle said. "I found the box and I tried to take Marggy home with me and caused you enough trouble, so you all run and hide and I will open the box!"

This was very kind of Mr. Doodle, for before he had been so very unkind to Marggy and her Mama and friends.

"Huh! I am not afraid," Raggedy Andy said. "I shall stand right here, and if a Magician or a Genei pops out of the box I will crack him on top of the head with this stubby stick."

"Indeed you shan't do that, Raggedy Andy," Raggedy Ann cried. "What if it should be a very kind hearted Magician, or a generous Genei who would help us find Marggy's Daddy? It wouldn't be nice to crack him on top of his head with the stubby stick!"

"Then I will not hit him on top of his head with the stick," Raggedy Andy agreed. "But just the same, I shall stay right here while Mr. Doodle opens the shiny box."

"Then we will all stay," Marggy's Mama said.

Mr. Doodle was just about to open the lid of the shiny box when Raggedy Ann cried, "Wait a moment! Before you open the box, try twisting the black knobs with the white numbers on them."

Everyone held their breaths while Mr. Doodle twisted the black knobs. "SQUEEEE—AWK—EEEE!"

"It sounds like you are pinching him when you twist the knobs!" Raggedy Andy said. Mr. Doodle twisted the knobs again and a voice from the box said, "Kay—dee—kay—aye," and then there came the tinkle of a piano.

"Someone lives in the box!" Raggedy Ann cried. "They are playing the piano."

"Yes! That's it, Raggedy Ann," Raggedy Andy said. "It is some little creature's home!"

"No it isn't!" a voice in back of Raggedy Ann said, and when they looked, our friends saw a little boy standing there and his eyes danced with merriment.

"How do you know?" Mr. Doodle asked.

"Because it is my box!" the boy replied, "I made it myself!"

"Then you must be a Magician, or a Fairy, or something!" Marggy's Mama said.

"Oh! Not at all," the little boy replied. "Almost any boy can make a box like that if he care to do so!"

"Well! It is my box now!" Mr. Doodle said as he picked up the shiny box and held it tightly under his arm.

"Why the idea, Mr. Doodle! It isn't your box at all!" Marggy's Mama cried.

"Yes it is!" Mr. Doodle shouted, "I found it in a hollow tree and so that makes it mine. Don't you see?"

"Why, Mr. Doodle! I'm s'prised at you!" Raggedy Ann said. "The pretty shiny box belongs to the nice little boy and you must give it to him!"

"I'll run with it and then you can't catch me!" Mr. Doodle said as he started running. The little boy ran after Mr. Doodle and so did Raggedy Andy.

The little boy could not run as fast as Raggedy Andy, so Raggedy Andy caught hold of Mr. Doodle's coat tails and held him. Mr. Doodle pulled and pulled until one of his coat tails came off and let Raggedy Andy fall down.

"Now then you'll catch it, Raggedy Andy!" Mr. Doodle screamed. "I shall pull off your coat tail because you pulled off my coat tail!" And he jumped at Raggedy Andy.

"Ha, ha, ha, ha! I haven't any coat tails!"

"Then we will have to fight!" Mr. Doodle cried.

"All right!" and Raggedy Andy rolled up his sleeves.

Mr. Doodle and Raggedy Andy were just about to fight when Raggedy Ann came running up. "Here!" she cried, "You mustn't fight! It isn't nice to quarrel and fight like cats and dogs! Besides, the little boy has taken the shiny box and run home with it."

"It was really all my fault," Mr. Doodle said when Raggedy Andy said he was sorry he tore his coat. "If I had not been so selfish and had not tried to run away with the little boy's shiny box you would not have torn my coat even a speck!"

"What kind of a magic box do you think it really was, Mr. Doodle?" Raggedy Ann wished to know.

"It was a radio," Mr. Doodle replied. "Didn't you guess that? Almost any one would guess it the first pop!"

"We had better hurry on so that we can find Marggy's Daddy," said Raggedy Ann. "You know he has been lost for the longest, longest time."

"When you hunt for Marggy's Daddy, why don't you have Marggy stay at my house?" Mr. Doodle asked. "She will get tired walking so far with you."

"Now, Mr. Doodle!" Raggedy Ann shook her rag thumb at him. "You know very well that Marggy wants to go with us and you just want her to go home with you so that she will chop the wood and build the fires 'n everything; 'cause you are too lazy to do it yourself!"

"Whoever says I am lazy will have to fight like the paper Dragon and I fought," Mr. Doodle cried as he hopped to his feet.

Raggedy Andy did not want Mr. Doodle to fight Raggedy Ann so he started rolling up his sleeves to fight Mr. Doodle in Raggedy Ann's place when Mrs. Doodle came running up from behind the tree and took Mr. Doodle right by his ear.

"Now then, Mr. Doodle," she cried as she pulled him along, "You march right home with me! I'm tired of having you try to get someone else to do the work all the time. From now on, you must do it yourself, you lazy thing."

And Mrs. Doodle meant just what she said too, for as long as they watched, Mrs. Doodle still had hold of Mr. Doodle's ear and was making him step towards home as fast as he could go without falling down.

CHAPTER SIX

FINALLY our friends came to a great stone castle with large gates in front of it. At one side of the gate was a great big soldier with a long gun and at the other side of the gate was a great big soldier with a long sword. "You can't come through the gate!" the two soldiers shouted when they saw our friends.

"If you walk through the gate, I'll have to cut off your ears!" the soldier with the long sword cried.

"I haven't any ears," Raggedy Andy laughed.

"Besides, the gate doesn't open anyway," the soldier with the gun said.

"If they won't let us go through the gate, let's walk around it," Raggedy Ann said.

"There!" one soldier said to the other. "I knew they'd guess it!"

"How did you ever think to walk around the gate when you couldn't walk through it?" one soldier asked.

"Because there isn't any fence on the sides of the gate!" Raggedy Ann laughed. Then the door opened and all walked right into the castle.

When Raggedy Ann, who came last had entered the castle, the great door closed behind her. Then the rug they were standing upon tipped down, so that Raggedy Andy, Marggy and her Mama and Raggedy Ann all went scooting down a slippery slide. Down, down they went, ever so fast, under the castle and when they came to the end, there they were on the road with the castle in back of them.

"I'm glad we didn't have to stay in the castle," Raggedy Andy said. "For who knows? It might have been a magical castle and we might have had to stay there for ever and ever!"

At the side of the road sat an old man. He sat upon a hard stone and he was knitting sox. After they had all said, "Good morning" to the old man, Marggy's Mama asked him, "Is this a magician's castle?"

"Yes, indeed it is!" the old man replied. "I'm trying my best to get in, for the Magician has a very magical canary bird of mine which sings beautiful songs all day long."

"Maybe you can climb up the slippery slide."

"No, I can't do that!" the old man said. "For you see, the slippery slide is too steep and slippery. I'll tell you a secret though, if you promise not to tell anyone."

"We promise!" Marggy said.

"Well, the secret is this," the old man whispered. "I'm knitting sixteen pair of sox and when I have them finished I shall unravel them and tie a stone to one end of the yarn. Then I'll throw the stone up to one of the windows and the stone will go behind one of the iron bars in front of the window and bounce out again. Then I will let the stone pull the yarn down until it touches the ground. I'll tie a rope to the yarn and pull the rope up to the window, then I'll climb up there and get in. Isn't that a nice secret? Do not tell anyone!"

"Oh, no, we won't," Raggedy Ann said. "But," she added, "have you thought that if you used the yarn before you knitted it into sox, you wouldn't have the trouble of unraveling it?"

"Dear me, no! I never thought of that!" the old man replied. "I've been sitting here for nine months knitting the sox and I am on the last one!"

"And then, too," Raggedy Ann wanted to know. "Even if you climbed up to the window, how would you get through the iron bars?"

"I am afraid I did not think of that either!" the old man sighed.

"And have you thought that maybe you can walk right into the front door if you go around there?" Raggedy Andy asked.

"No sir! I never thought of that either!"

"Have you thought of eating since you started knitting the sox?" Marggy's Mama asked.

"Dear me! I've been so busy, I forgot that too!"

"Then I'll tell you what I would do if I were you," Marggy's Mama said as she gave the old man eight cream puffs and nine doughnuts. "I'd eat these, then I'd run home to my mama as fast as I could scamper."

"Oh, thank you!" the old man chuckled. "I'll run home to mama right away. I'd forgotten her. Maybe she will be hungry too." And away he went, lickity split through the woods.

"Well, well, well!" Raggedy Ann laughed as she watched the funny old man run away. "He has gone and left the sox he has been working on so long!"

Marggy's Mama picked up the sox and put them in her basket. "If we pass his house I will hand them to him."

"Here he comes running back!" Marggy cried. "Isn't he funny?"

"Hello!" he cried as he came up to our friends. "Do you know where I was running to? I was running as hard as I could through the woods when all of a sudden I wondered what I was running for. So I came back to ask you!"

"You were taking the doughnuts and cream puffs home to give to your mama," Marggy's Mama explained.

"Oh! So I was!" the funny old man said. "Well sir, I have eaten all the doughnuts and cream puffs!"

"That is too bad!" Raggedy Ann said. "For you told us your mama might be very hungry while you had been away nine months knitting the sox!"

"Dear me! So I did!" the old man admitted. "I must hurry back and get the sox and then hurry right home before I forget it!"

"Wait a moment!" Raggedy Ann cried as the funny old

man started to run, "Marggy's Mama has your sox in her basket, so you will not have to run back!"

"Then I must run home as fast as I can and see how my mama is, she may be very hungry."

"Now we will hurry after him and see where his home is for if he has been away for nine months, his mama will be very, very hungry and will like our doughnuts and cream puffs," Raggedy Ann said thoughtfully.

Raggedy Ann and Raggedy Andy and Marggy and her Mama caught hold of hands and ran after the funny little man until they saw him run into a queer little house. Smoke was coming out of the chimney and when they walked up to the door a nice little old lady came to meet them. "Come right in!" she cried cheerily. "My husband told me you might be along pretty soon, and as I have been making some candy covered cup cakes, I would like you to come in and have some with lemonade." And she took Raggedy Ann and her friends into the dining room and gave them all they could eat and drink. When they had finished, the funny old man's wife asked, "Why has Mr. Felix got that piece of red yarn tied around his nose?"

Raggedy Ann laughed. "Why! Mrs. Felix, hasn't he told you?"

"No!" Mrs. Felix replied. "He had forgotten by the time he reached home!"

"Then I'll tell you why he has it tied around his nose," Raggedy Ann said. "We met him back by the castle and gave him some cream puffs and doughnuts to bring home to you, for he told us he had not been home for nine months. You see, we thought you might be hungry, so we tied the yarn around his nose so he wouldn't forget to run right straight home!"

"Dear me!" Mrs. Felix sighed, "I do not know what to do for Mr. Felix. He forgets everything. Why just an hour ago I sent him down to the grocery to get a loaf of bread and a pound of bacon and you found him sitting along the road. I guess he forgot that I sent him to the store!"

"No! I didn't forget to go to the store," Mr. Felix said. "But I forgot what you sent me for, so I bought fifteen pairs of sox and some yarn and knitting needles."

"And he told us he was knitting the sox himself!" Marggy said.

"Dear me, what can I do with him?" Mrs. Felix cried. "When he was a little boy he used to tell fibs and as an excuse for telling fibs he would say, 'I forgot' until he told it so many times he finally got so he really did forget, and now he cannot remember anything!"

"My goodness!" Raggedy Ann said, "I am glad there are not many children like him; for think how queer it would be to have them grow up and not be able to remember anything!"

"Maybe you can cure him of forgetting by making him go without his supper and see if he is hungry enough in the morning to remember it. Then if he forgets, make him go without his dinner and see if he forgets that!" Marggy said.

"Oh my! He would never forget anything like that!" Mrs. Felix laughed. "It's just the other things he forgets."

"Then I believe a good paddywhacking would be the best thing for him," Raggedy Ann laughed.

"Just the thing!" Mrs. Felix cried as she seized the pancake paddle and before he had time to run, Mr. Felix found himself across Mrs. Felix's knees and was being paddywhacked real hard.

"Now will you remember not to forget?" Mrs. Felix asked.

"Indeed I will!" Mr. Felix replied as he wiped his forehead with his pocket hanky, and to prove that he remembered not to forget, Mr. Felix repeated every single thing he had told Raggedy Ann back near the castle in the woods.

"I'll bet a nickel I never, never forget again," Mr. Felix said. "Never, never, for it isn't any fun being paddywhacked with a pancake paddle, I can tell you!"

"We asked Mr. Felix who lived in the castle and he told us a Magician lived there," Raggedy Ann said.

"Yes, that is true," Mrs. Felix said. "Didn't you run in to see him when you passed?"

"We went in," Raggedy Andy laughed, "But we hardly stepped inside the door before we slid down a slippery slide and went scooting out on this side!"

"Then if the Magician is a kindly Magician, what do you say if we go to see him? He may be able to tell us where Marggy's Daddy is," Raggedy Ann said.

Marggy and her Mama thought this would be a good plan. "And," Marggy's Mama said. "Even if we should slide down the slippery slide again, it is a lot of fun!"

So thanking Mrs. Felix for the nice cup cakes and lemonade, our friends returned to the gate where the two soldiers stood guard.

'Hello!" Raggedy Ann cried in her cheeriest voice. "We wish to go in and visit the Magician."

"Alright!" one of the soldiers said. "But you will have to walk around the gate, because you know it doesn't open!"

"Thank you!" Raggedy Ann said. "When we went in the door before, we dropped through the floor and went scooting down a slippery slide, way under the castle!"

One of the soldiers came up to Raggedy Ann and whispered, "Don't tell a soul, Raggedy Ann!" he said. "It's a secret. When you go in the castle, you must go around to the side door. Everyone who goes in the front door, falls down and scoots on the slippery slide!"

"Did you ever see Marggy's Daddy walking along here?" Raggedy Andy asked one of the soldiers.

"I don't believe so," the soldier replied. "But when you go inside, you ask the Magician. He knows ever and ever so much!"

So the Raggedys thanked the kind soldiers and walking around to the side door rang a little bell. In answer to the bell, the door was opened a crack and a long nose was poked out. "Who is it?" the owner of the long nose asked.

Raggedy Ann named over all in the little party, then said, "We wish to ask the Magician if he knows where Marggy's Daddy is, her Daddy has been lost a long, long time."

"Wait a moment!" the long nosed person said. "I will run and ask the Magician!"

Presently the long nosed man returned. "The Magician says that he knows where Marggy's Daddy is, but he will not tell unless you do something for him!"

"What does he wish us to do for him?" Raggedy Andy wanted to know.

"The Magician will tell you!" the long nosed man said as he opened the door and they followed him down a long hall.

In a large room, sitting upon a throne was a queer little man with long whiskers. This was the Magician who owned the castle. He greeted our friends by tipping his crown. "Hello!" he said. "If you want to find Marggy's Daddy, you must do something for me first! That's the way they always do things in fairy tales."

"But this isn't a fairy tale," Raggedy Ann said.

"Of course it is!" the magician laughed. "How can two rag dolls walk and talk unless it is a fairy tale. So I want you to go out and bring me back a dragon, then maybe I can think of something else for you to do!"

Raggedy Ann and Raggedy Andy whispered together, then Raggedy Andy asked, "If I bring you a dragon, what will you do with him?"

"I do not know," the Magician answered. "I never had a dragon, but I've read of them in fairy tales and every great Magician really needs a dragon around his castle. I 'spect though, I would have to keep him in a chicken coop to keep him from eating people!"

"I believe I can bring you a dragon," Raggedy Andy said. "But it will be a very nice, kind Dragon who does not eat people, so if you will promise that you won't put him in a cage, but let him live here in the castle with you until he gets ready to leave, I will go and hunt for him."

"All right," the Magician promised.

So Raggedy Andy filled his pockets with doughnuts from Marggy's Mama's basket and started out the door.

"Wait a moment!" the Magician cried. "You mustn't go to fight a Dragon without a sword." And he handed Raggedy Andy a wooden sword.

"Do you really believe Raggedy Andy will bring back a Dragon?" the Magician asked as he motioned Raggedy Ann and Marggy and her Mama to take seats near him.

"I wouldn't be a bit surprised if he brought back a nice fat Dragon," Raggedy Ann laughed and winked one of her shoe button eyes at Marggy's Mama. Then the Magician clapped his hands and two servants came in with trays of ice cream sodas.

When Raggedy Andy left Raggedy Ann and Marggy and her Mama at the castle of the Magician, he ran with his wooden sword through the woods back to where they left the paper Dragon. "Yoo hoo!" Raggedy Andy called in his loudest Raggedy voice. But call as loud as he could, the paper Dragon did not reply.

"That's funny," Raggedy Andy cried. "I wonder what has become of the Dragon?"

"I'll tell you where the paper Dragon is," a little Gnome said as he walked up to Raggedy Andy. "After you left, Mr. Doodle came and dragged the paper Dragon home."

"Dear me," Raggedy Andy sighed. "Now we shall never be able to find Marggy's Daddy."

"I'm afraid not!" the little Gnome said. "For I heard Mr. Doodle tell Mrs. Doodle that he would make a chicken coop out of the Dragon."

"If Mr. Doodle has broken up that lovely, kindly, paper Dragon to make a chicken coop, I don't know what I shall do to Mr. Doodle," promised Raggedy Andy.

"Then maybe you had better hurry to Mr. Doodle's house as soon as you can," advised the little Gnome. "If that sword was given you by the Magician," the little Gnome added, "It must be a magic sword, so get on it just like you would a hobby horse and see if it doesn't carry you along faster than you can run on your cotton stuffed legs."

Raggedy Andy was greatly surprised, but when he straddled the magic wooden sword and held his feet off the ground, the wooden sword went sailing along above the ground a lot faster than Raggedy Andy could run. And while the wooden sword carried him along toward Mr. Doodle's house, Raggedy Andy ate the doughnuts he had brought along, because he knew if he had to fight Mr. Doodle he would need lots of strength. And of course doughnuts are very good to give you strength, if you do not eat too many of them.

Raggedy Andy felt sure he could coax the kind paper Dragon to return with him to the Magician's castle.

The magic sword soon carried Raggedy Andy right to Mr. Doodle's front door.

Raggedy Andy took the wooden sword and knocked on Mr. Doodle's front door. Bang! Bang! Bang! But no one answered. So Raggedy Andy walked out in back of the fence and there was Mr. and Mrs. Doodle and the paper Dragon.

Mr. Doodle had tied the paper Dragon to stakes and was trying to drive all his chickens in the paper Dragon's mouth, but the chickens did not care to go in the paper Dragon, because they thought the Dragon would eat them, and the paper Dragon did not wish the chickens inside his paper body any more than the chickens wanted to be there, so the paper Dragon tried his best to growl and frighten the chickens. Mr. Doodle had put a stick in the paper Dragon's mouth and this kept the Dragon from growling as loud as Dragons usually growl.

Mrs. Doodle shooed the chickens and Mr. Doodle shooed the chickens and the paper Dragon did not like it even a teeny weeny bit, so you bet he was very glad when Raggedy Andy walked up and asked in a loud stern voice, "What are you doing with that Dragon, Mr. Doodle?"

"I'm making a chicken coop out of the Dragon, that's what!" Mr. Doodle replied.

"And I've come to rescue the Dragon, that's what, Mr. Doodle!" Raggedy Andy said.

"But I shan't let you rescue him!" Mr. Doodle shouted quite loud.

"And I say, I SHALL RESCUE HIM!" Raggedy Andy shouted still louder.

Neither one knew what to do next until Mrs. Doodle went in the house and brought out tea and cinnamon toast. "I will think of a way to fight pretty soon," Mr. Doodle promised as he passed the tea and toast to Raggedy Andy.

After they had finished eating and had wiped the cinnamon from around their mouths, Raggedy Andy knew it was time to rescue the Dragon, so he said to Mr. Doodle, "Maybe you

don't know it, but this wooden sword I carry is a very magical wooden sword. The Magician gave it to me, so that I could bring the Dragon to his castle. Now if I should crack you on top of your head with the sword, it will make a large bump and you will not be able to wear your hat, it will hurt so much."

"Then maybe I had better let you rescue the Dragon," said Mr. Doodle.

"I believe that will be the best way to do," Raggedy Andy replied. "And anyway the chickens do not care to go inside a Dragon chicken coop."

"Indeed, that is true," Mr. Doodle agreed. So Raggedy Andy cut all the ropes which held the paper Dragon, and the paper Dragon was so thankful, he wiggled all over and would have licked Raggedy Andy's hand, only whoever made the paper Dragon, forgot to make him a paper tongue, so he couldn't even lick a postage stamp.

"We'd better be going," Raggedy Andy told the Dragon. "The Magician wished me to bring you to the castle."

"I'd rather be a chicken coop than have the Magician shut me up in a cage," Mr. Doodle teased.

"Don't pay any attention to him," Raggedy Andy whispered. "He's just peevish because I rescued you."

"I know it," the Dragon laughed. "And even if the Magician shuts me up in a cage, I'll go with you anyway, because I shall be very glad to help you find Marggy's Daddy."

Raggedy Andy and the paper Dragon went through the woods towards the Magician's castle. "It won't be very long until we get there," said Raggedy Andy.

"Maybe if you would ride upon my head, we could go a little faster," the Dragon suggested. So Raggedy Andy climbed upon the Dragon's head and the Dragon wiggled through the woods, lickety split. The paper Dragon was very long; his head was very far in front of his tail, and so when the Dragon suddenly stopped, Raggedy Andy flew right off the Dragon's head and lit upon the soft ground.

"Why did you stop?" Raggedy Andy asked.

"I believe my tail is fastened on a stick," the Dragon replied.

Raggedy Andy could not see whether the Dragon's tail was fastened on a stick or not, so he ran back to look.

"Ha! Ha! Ha! That's the time I fooled you!" cried Mr. Doodle.

Yes, sir, it was him! He had run after Raggedy Andy and the Dragon and now, there he sat upon a stone and laughed.

"Why did you fasten the Dragon's tail on a stick?" Raggedy Andy asked.

"I didn't fasten his tail to a stick!" shouted Mr. Doodle. "I want the paper Dragon for a chicken coop, so I put salt on his tail!"

"Dear me! that was very unkind of you!" Raggedy Andy cried, for you see he knew very well that the way to catch Dragons is to put salt upon their tails.

But it isn't nice to have someone else put salt upon a Dragon's tail when that Dragon is a nice friendly Dragon, for a Dragon can't even wiggle a smidgin when it has salt upon its tail. Raggedy Andy sat down beside Mr. Doodle and tried to think of a way to rescue the Dragon again. And while he sat there and thought, he nibbled on one of his doughnuts, and seeing that Mr. Doodle looked hungry, Raggedy Andy gave

Mr. Doodle a doughnut too. For, it is best to be generous and unselfish, even to those who are unkind to us.

"If I don't take the Dragon to the Magician's castle, the Magician will not tell us where Marggy's Daddy is," Raggedy Andy told Mr. Doodle.

"I know it," Mr. Doodle replied as he nibbled the doughnut. "But if you take the Dragon to the Magician's castle, then don't you see, I shall be unable to make the paper Dragon into a chicken coop."

"The paper Dragon will not make a very good chicken coop," Raggedy Andy said.

"Cause why?" Mr. Doodle wanted to know.

"Because," Raggedy Andy explained. "Some time when the chickens are walking into the paper Dragon's mouth, the paper Dragon will bite them."

"Ha, ha, ha!" Mr. Doodle laughed. "I'll prop the Dragon's mouth open with a long stick, so that he won't bite the chickens."

"If you do that, Mr. Doodle, all the chickens will walk right out of his mouth, cause it will always be open."

But just as Raggedy Andy and Mr. Doodle finished eating their doughnuts Raggedy Andy had an idea. "When Mr. Doodle put salt upon the Dragon's tail, the Dragon could not move," he thought to himself. "So if I want to rescue the nice Dragon, I must brush the salt off his tail!"

So Raggedy Andy said to Mr. Doodle, "How much salt did you put on the Dragon's tail, Mr. Doodle?"

"You can see how much," Mr. Doodle replied as he pointed to the pile of salt on the Dragon's tail.

"Why didn't you put more on his tail?"

"Because that is all the salt I had with me!"

This was what Raggedy Andy wanted to know for Raggedy Andy knew if he brushed the salt off the Dragon's tail, the Dragon would be able to wiggle away through the woods.

"You stay here and eat this doughnut," Raggedy Andy said to Mr. Doodle. "While I go up to the Dragon's head and see if he feels all right."

"Do not stay too long," Mr. Doodle said. "For just as soon as I eat this doughnut, I shall take the Dragon home."

So Raggedy Andy ran up to the Dragon's head and said to him, "Now if I can, I shall fool Mr. Doodle and brush all the salt off your tail. So as soon as you feel all the salt brushed off, you must wiggle through the woods to the Magician's castle just as fast as you can wiggle, and I will hop upon the magic wooden sword the Magician gave me and we will escape from Mr. Doodle."

The paper Dragon promised that he would wiggle as fast as he had ever wiggled before, so Raggedy Andy walked back to Mr. Doodle at the Dragon's tail.

"So you think that you can fool me some way and brush the salt off the Dragon's tail, do you?" Mr. Doodle asked when Raggedy Andy came up.

"How in the world did you guess it?" Raggedy Andy asked.

Mr. Doodle laughed. "When you talked to the paper Dragon's head, I listened at his tail, and because the paper Dragon is hollow all the way down I could hear just as plain as if you talked through a pipe."

"Then I guess there is no way for me to fool you, Mr. Doodle," Raggedy Andy said in a sad voice.

"You can't fool me very easy, that is sure," Mr. Doodle replied as he brushed the doughnut crumbs away from his mouth.

"Did you ever see a hippopotamus up in a tree, Mr. Doodle?" Raggedy Andy asked as he looked up in the tree above him.

"No! I never did, Raggedy Andy! And what's more, I never will see a hippopotamus up in a tree!" Mr. Doodle replied.

"And that is true, Mr. Doodle, if you never look up in trees," Raggedy Andy said. "For how can you expect to see a hippopotamus up in a tree, if you do not look?" And as Mr. Doodle was very anxious to see a hippopotamus up a tree, he looked up.

"I don't see him at all," he said.

"Neither do I, Mr. Doodle." And as he said this, Raggedy Andy reached over and brushed every speck of salt off the Dragon's tail, and away went the paper Dragon through the woods towards the Magician's castle as fast as he could wiggle. When Raggedy Andy jumped upon the magic wooden sword and told the magic wooden sword to follow the paper Dragon, the magic wooden sword did not budge a speck.

"Ha! Ha! Ha!" Mr. Doodle laughed when Raggedy Andy looked surprised. "The magic wooden sword will not carry you away, because I tied a string to the wooden sword and to that stump!"

"If I only had a knife, I would cut the string!" Raggedy Andy laughed although he felt very disappointed.

"Now you have made me lose the paper Dragon," Mr. Doodle said. "So instead of making a chicken coop out of the paper Dragon, as I wished to do, I shall take you home and make you build me a chicken coop out of boards!"

Raggedy Andy did not know what else to say, so he said to Mr. Doodle, "I don't believe I can go back to your house and build a chicken coop today, because I'm too busy."

But Mr. Doodle only laughed real loud. "It won't do any good for you to tell me you are too busy today to build me a chicken coop!" Mr. Doodle cried as he dragged Raggedy Andy home and tied him with a string near the wood pile. "Now while I go in the house and eat my dinner, you can start building the chicken coop." And he gave Raggedy Andy a saw and a hammer and a lot of nails. "And if you don't have the chicken coop finished when I get through my dinner I shall paddywhack you," Mr. Doodle promised.

So Raggedy Andy sawed the boards and nailed them together. Then he happened to think, "I can saw the string in two and run to where Mr. Doodle has the wooden sword tied to the stump and saw the string which holds the magic wooden sword." Raggedy Andy had just finished sawing the string with which Mr. Doodle had tied him, when Mr. Doodle came running out of his house.

"That's the time I fooled you!" Raggedy Andy cried as he ran with the saw through the woods. When he came to where the magic wooden sword was tied to the stump, Raggedy Andy cut the strings. And just as Mr. Doodle ran up to catch him, Raggedy Andy jumped on the magic sword and cried, "Magic wooden sword, carry me after the paper Dragon to the Magician's castle!" And the magic wooden sword flew over the ground so fast Mr. Doodle was left far behind.

CHAPTER SEVEN

RAGGEDY Andy soon reached the large gate in front of the Magician's castle. There stood the two soldiers; one with a real long sword and the other with a real long gun and they held up their hands and cried, "Stop!"

"Did you see a Dragon come by this way?" Raggedy Andy asked the two soldiers.

"Yes!" the soldiers replied. "The Dragon frightened us so we ran and hid and the Dragon climbed right up to the window and wiggled in the castle. Maybe by this time the Dragon has eaten the Magician."

"I shall go inside and see!" Raggedy Andy replied.

But the two soldiers said, "We will not let you go inside the castle and be eaten by the Dragon!"

But Raggedy Andy looked back and saw that Mr. Doodle was running after him as hard as he could come, so Raggedy Andy just whispered to the magic wooden sword and the magic wooden sword carried Raggedy Andy right over the two soldiers' heads and over the gate, just as Mr. Doodle came running up.

"Catch him!" Mr. Doodle cried, but of course he was too late. The wooden sword carried Raggedy Andy right to the castle door, but the door was locked and Raggedy Andy could not get in.

Mr. Doodle kicked so much, the two soldiers could not hold him so just as Mr. Doodle came running up, Raggedy Andy cried to the wooden sword, "Get up, wooden sword, fly up through the window in the castle!"

Once inside the Magician's castle, Raggedy Andy went down stairs to the room where the Magician usually sat upon his throne. But everything was topsy turvy. The chairs were turned over and the Magician's throne was upside down.

"Dear me!" Raggedy Andy exclaimed as he ran his rag hand up through his red yarn hair, "I wonder what could have happened?" So Raggedy Andy went all through the castle until he found the Dragon.

"Well!" said Raggedy Andy, "I'm glad that I found you. I had a hard time escaping from Mr. Doodle. He dragged me home and made me start building his chicken coop, but while he was eating his dinner, I sawed the string with which he had tied me and escaped."

The Dragon only looked at Raggedy Andy in a funny way, but did not say anything.

"Have you seen the Magician and Raggedy Ann and Marggy and her Mama?" Raggedy Andy asked the Dragon.

"Mumble, mumble, mumble," was all the Dragon replied, for he was trying to talk without opening his mouth.

"Now!" Raggedy Andy said as he pointed his rag thumb at the Dragon. "Tell me! Did you swallow the Magician?"

The Dragon nodded his head up and down and Raggedy Andy knew then that the Dragon had swallowed them.

"Open your mouth!" Raggedy Andy told the Dragon. So the Dragon opened his mouth and the Magician and Raggedy Ann and Marggy and her Mama came walking out.

"You must leave my castle right away!" the Magician cried. "I won't have a Dragon around here swallowing people like this Dragon did."

"But he is only a paper Dragon, Mr. Magician!"

"I know he is now!" the Magician replied. "But how was I to know he was made out of paper when he came wiggling through the window and swallowed all of us?"

"Why did you swallow them?" Raggedy Andy asked the Dragon.

"I did not know what to do until you came," the Dragon replied. "So I just swallowed everybody and waited until you came."

"And now you must take the Dragon and leave!" the Magician cried and pushed them all outside.

"Oh, dear!" Raggedy Andy cried. "Now that the Dragon has made the Magician so peevish, he will never tell us where Marggy's Daddy is and we shall never find him. And, besides, Mr. Doodle is out here fighting with the two soldiers and if he wins the fight, he will capture the Dragon and we will have to rescue the Dragon all over again!"

"Let us hurry away while Mr. Doodle and the two soldiers are still fighting," Raggedy Ann suggested. "Perhaps Mr. Doodle will not see us!" So they all started to run. But Mr. Doodle, just as soon as he caught sight of the Dragon and Raggedy Ann and Andy trying to escape, quit fighting with the two soldiers and ran after our friends, and because Marggy and her Mama could not run very fast Mr. Doodle soon caught the Dragon's tail and stopped him. Mr. Doodle started to drag the Dragon towards his house, but Raggedy Ann and Raggedy Andy and Marggy and her Mama caught hold of the Dragon's head and pulled the other way.

Mr. Doodle pulled and pulled and our friends pulled and pulled until they all pulled so hard, the paper Dragon tore right in two. And Mr. Doodle was pulling so hard and our friends were pulling so hard, when the paper Dragon was torn in two, they all fell over backwards.

"Now then you have done it, Mr. Doodle," Raggedy Ann cried as she jumped to her feet and ran back to Mr. Doodle. "Aren't you ashamed of yourself?"

"No I am not!" Mr. Doodle replied. "If you had not pulled upon the Dragon's head, he would not have torn in two!"

Raggedy Andy took the Dragon's tail away from Mr. Doodle. "I have a good mind to box your ears, Mr. Doodle!" Raggedy Andy said.

"Ha! Ha! Ha!" Mr. Doodle laughed. "Your hands are made of cloth and stuffed with cotton, so it wouldn't hurt if you did!"

"Then I shall try mine!" Marggy's Mama cried. And if Raggedy Ann had not stopped her, Marggy's Mama would have given Mr. Doodle a box on the ear which he would have remembered for a long time.

The paper Dragon looked very sad, for he could not wiggle at all with his tail torn off and he wished to go with our friends on their journey in search of Marggy's Daddy. And then, too, when the paper Dragon was torn in two, that let the air whistle right through his paper body each time he opened his mouth. Marggy's Mama would have liked to paddywhack Mr. Doodle, but she knew that would do no good. "We must fix the paper Dragon together some way," she said.

Raggedy Ann had mended a hole in the paper Dragon's side once before with the cream from a cream puff and a pretty colored Sunday newspaper, but now they only had

chocolate cake, doughnuts and cookies left, for they had eaten all the cream puffs. Raggedy Andy suggested that by using little sticks as pins, they might pin the Dragon's tail together. "Of course he will still be torn!" Raggedy Andy said, "but if we can fix him together so that he can travel with us, maybe along the way, we will find a way to glue him together!"

So they all gathered little twigs and with these they pinned the Dragon's tail to the front part of his body. Even Mr. Doodle helped. Raggedy Ann and Raggedy Andy did not care to have Mr. Doodle go with them in search of Marggy's Daddy, nor did they wish him to take the Dragon back home for a chicken coop, but they were too polite to tell him so.

"It is too bad Mr. Doodle tore the tail from the paper Dragon," Raggedy Ann said, " 'cause now the paper Dragon can not wiggle along very fast."

"I'm glad he can't wiggle along very fast," Mr. Doodle laughed. "For I will follow you and just as soon as you find someone to mend the Dragon, I will take him away from you and use him for a chicken coop."

Raggedy Andy did not reply to Mr. Doodle but he thought, "When we have the nice paper Dragon mended, I will not let you take him away from us!"

So the Dragon wiggled along very slowly so as not to unfasten his tail and Raggedy Ann and Raggedy Andy and Marggy and her Mama walked beside him. Although they did not want him with them, Mr. Doodle went along. After a while they came to a funny little house. There was only one room down stairs and all the other rooms were built right on top of each other.

CHAPTER EIGHT

"WE will go inside and get something to eat," Mr. Doodle said. "I pulled so hard on the Dragon's tail, I am hungry." And without even knocking on the door, Mr. Doodle walked right inside the funny little house.

"You should not walk into any one's house without knocking, Mr. Doodle," Raggedy Ann told him.

But Mr. Doodle only laughed, "Ha! ha, ha!" like that, only a great deal louder, and went in anyway.

"Now that he is inside, we have a good chance to run away from him!" Raggedy Andy said.

The others thought this would be a good plan because Mr. Doodle had always been so mean to them, but when they heard Mr. Doodle squealing ever so loudly, they waited to see what was happening. My goodness! Didn't Mr. Doodle squeal? He squealed so loud and so long, Raggedy Andy said, "I 'spect I had better go inside and see why Mr. Doodle squeals!" Raggedy Andy was very polite, so he knocked upon the door.

"Come in!" someone said in a cheery voice, so Raggedy Andy walked in and saw Mr. Doodle standing with his long nose caught in a cupboard door and there stood a little man watching Mr. Doodle.

"Do you know," the little man said, "Mr. Doodle walked right into my house without knocking and poked his nose in my cupboard; and the cupboard door flew shut and caught him. It serves him right for snooping in other people's things!"

"Indeed it does!" Raggedy Andy agreed. "But Mr. Doodle is squealing so loud, maybe it would be best to open the cupboard door so that he can pull his nose out."

So the little man opened the cupboard door and Mr. Doodle sat down upon the floor and held his nose.

"Now all of you come inside," the little man said to Raggedy Ann and Marggy and her Mama. "And we will have something to eat, for I know you must all be hungry!" So he gave them chocolate cake and cookies and ice cream and dill pickles and milk and it was a very nice dinner. Mr. Doodle's nose hurt so much he could not eat anything and he was very sorry that he had not knocked upon the door instead of walking in and snooping around.

The little man filled Marggy's Mama's basket with lots of good things to eat, "So you will not get hungry along the way," he said, then turning to Mr. Doodle the little man said, "Mr. Doodle, if I were you, I would run right straight home—Raggedy Ann and Raggedy Andy and Marggy and her Mama do not care to have you go with them. Besides, you are so ill mannered you will always be getting into trouble. You had better run home, I believe your Mama is calling you."

"I shall not go home until I get the Dragon!" Mr. Doodle shouted, much louder than was necessary. "Because why? Because I intend making him into a chicken coop!"

"Mr. Doodle pulled the nice tail off of the kind paper Dragon," Raggedy Ann told the little man. "We had to mend his tail with little sticks."

"Yes!" Mr. Doodle cried. "And as soon as we get some glue to mend the Dragon's tail, I shall take the Dragon away from Raggedy Ann and Raggedy Andy!"

"I will give Raggedy Andy some glue," the little man said. "And sometime when Mr. Doodle is asleep, Raggedy Andy can mend the Dragon's tail and all get upon the Dragon's back and escape from Mr. Doodle."

Raggedy Andy put the bottle of glue in his pocket and then the little man took everyone except Mr. Doodle up to the top room. Mr. Doodle wanted to go with them, but the little man said, "No sir, Mr. Doodle, you must stay down stairs while we look out over the woods and see if we can see Marggy's Daddy."

So Mr. Doodle had to sit downstairs and twiddle his thumbs while the others went up and looked out over the deep, deep woods.

"Did Marggy's Daddy have four fingers and a thumb upon each hand?" the little man asked as they looked out the window.

"Yes!" Marggy's Mama said.

"And did he have two eyes and one nose and one mouth and two ears and hair on top of his head and two feet?" the little man asked.

"Yes!" Marggy's Mama replied.

"Then," said the little man, "I'll bet a nickel your Daddy was here, for a man who answered his description came here and asked for something to eat yesterday."

The little man told them the direction Marggy's Daddy had gone, so they thanked him and went downstairs.

"Oh, dear me!" Raggedy Ann cried when she walked out the door. "Mr. Doodle has gone and he has taken the Dragon with him!"

"Well! We must run after him and take the Dragon away from him!" Raggedy Andy said.

So Raggedy Ann and Raggedy Andy and Marggy and her Mama ran after Mr. Doodle until they came up to him.

"Now!" cried Raggedy Ann, as she stamped her rag foot. "Why did you take the Dragon away from us, Mr. Doodle? Just you tell me that!"

"Because I wish to make a chicken coop out of him! That's what and I shall not tell you again, Miss Raggedy Ann, and besides, I grew tired waiting for you back in the funny little house! I know that I can mend the Dragon's tail with glue a whole lot better than Raggedy Andy can, and I shall do it as soon as I get home!"

"You know perfectly well, Mr. Doodle the poor paper Dragon does not care to be made into a chicken coop and besides, when you capture him, can't you see that delays us? How do you 'spect us to find Marggy's Daddy when you act this way?" Raggedy Ann said.

"I shall take the paper Dragon home anyway!" Mr. Doodle howled as he pulled the paper Dragon.

"If we catch hold of the paper Dragon and pull back we will only pull the Dragon in two again," Raggedy Ann said to Marggy's Mama. "What had we better do?"

"I had better fight Mr. Doodle and see which one wins the paper Dragon," said Raggedy Andy.

"Why not let me fight with Mr. Doodle?" the Dragon said in a wheezy voice.

"That would be silly," Mr. Doodle replied. "I have already captured the Dragon, so he cannot fight with me."

"That is quite true," Raggedy Ann agreed. "I guess Raggedy Andy will have to fight with Mr. Doodle, but you must promise not to fight too hard."

So after Raggedy Andy and Mr. Doodle had both promised to fight real easy-like, they rolled up their sleeves. Mr. Doodle had the best of it for a long time because he could stick out his tongue at Raggedy Andy, but Raggedy Andy could not stick out his tongue at Mr. Doodle because Raggedy Andy's mouth was just painted on and he did not have a tongue. Of course, Raggedy Andy would not have stuck out his tongue at Mr. Doodle, even if he had a tongue, for that is a very rude thing to do, as everyone knows. But after awhile Raggedy Andy tweeked Mr. Doodle's nose and because Raggedy Andy's nose was painted upon his face, Mr. Doodle could not tweek Raggedy Andy's nose. Mr. Doodle sat down on a log and howled and then, of course, Raggedy Andy won the fight.

"Hurrah! Now we can mend the paper Dragon with the glue the little man gave us and go in search of Marggy's Daddy!" Raggedy Ann cried as she jumped up and down.

After walking a long time Marggy's Mama opened the basket of lunch. "Shall we give Mr. Doodle any?" Marggy's Mama asked. "He has treated us so mean he does not deserve any!"

Really, Mr. Doodle did not deserve any, but he looked so hungry, Raggedy Ann and Raggedy Andy, after whispering together, told Mr. Doodle to sit between them on the log and they gave him some of the doughnuts. After they had finished eating the doughnuts Raggedy Andy said, "Now we can travel in search of Marggy's Daddy and Mr. Doodle cannot follow us."

"Indeed, I can!" Mr. Doodle cried. "Whenever you start, I shall start with you."

Raggedy Ann and Raggedy Andy said to Marggy and her Mama, "Come! Let's hurry!" and they walked away leaving Mr. Doodle sitting on the log.

Mr. Doodle had a very queer look upon his face, because he did not know why he could not follow them.

"I took some of the glue and put it upon the log between Raggedy Ann and me," Raggedy Andy explained to Marggy and her Mama. "And when Mr. Doodle sat upon the glue, of course he stuck fast so now we can mend the paper Dragon and ride upon his back. Then Mr. Doodle will not be able to run and catch up with us and we will soon find Marggy's Daddy!"

It had only taken Raggedy Ann and Raggedy Andy two minutes to mend the Dragon's tail with the glue the little man has given them and it was such fine glue, it stuck very fast. It was lots of fun riding through the woods upon the paper Dragon's back because the Dragon wiggled along so smoothly. And our friends could not feel a bump even when the Dragon wiggled over large stones.

"I'm glad we have escaped from Mr. Doodle," the Dragon said as he carried his friends along upon his back. "For if we do not have Mr. Doodle bothering us all the time I am sure we will soon find Marggy's Daddy."

Raggedy Ann and Raggedy Andy and Marggy and her Mama felt so happy they laughed and sang songs as the Dragon carried them through the lovely woods.

CHAPTER NINE

AFTER awhile Raggedy Ann turned to say something to Raggedy Andy, and there coming behind them was Mr. Doodle. "Oh dear! Here comes Mr. Doodle!" Raggedy Ann said.

Raggedy Andy turned and looked. "My goodness!" he cried. "I forgot and left my magic wooden sword and now Mr. Doodle is riding upon the magic wooden sword and will soon catch up with us!"

The Dragon, on hearing this wiggled faster than ever, so fast that the trees and bushes seemed to whiz by, but the paper dragon could not go as fast as the magic wooden sword and pretty soon Mr. Doodle caught up with them.

"Stop, or I'll cut off the dragon's tail!" Mr. Doodle shouted to Raggedy Ann and Raggedy Andy.

"You cannot use the magic sword to cut off the dragon's tail while you are riding upon the wooden sword," Raggedy Andy laughed.

"Of course I can't when I am riding upon the wooden sword," Mr. Doodle shouted. "But unless you stop, I shall climb from the wooden sword to the dragon's back and then cut off his tail!"

There isn't anything to do except stop," Raggedy Ann

said. "We do not care to have Mr. Doodle cut off your tail again," she said to the dragon.

"How did you get free from where you were glued to the log?" Raggedy Andy asked Mr. Doodle.

"When I saw you leaving me alone on the log I wiggled and twisted as hard as I could, trying to get loose, but I could not get free. Then I grew angry and cried and the

tears ran down my nose onto the log and melted the glue When I got loose, didn't I laugh!"

"Why did you laugh, silly?" Marggy's mama wished to know, as she opened her basket and gave cookies to everyone.

"I laughed because I saw that Raggedy Andy had left his magic wooden sword and I knew I would soon catch up with you! That's why I laughed!"

"Sit down on the log beside Raggedy Andy and me and have some lunch, Mr. Doodle. We do not believe in being unkind to you even if you have been mean to us," Raggedy Ann said.

Mr. Doodle looked carefully to see if Raggedy Andy had put more glue upon the log. "If you try to fool me again I shall give you a hard thump, Raggedy Andy," Mr. Doodle said.

"Give Mr. Doodle a handful of cookies," Raggedy Andy said to Marggy's mama and when Marggy's mama had done this Raggedy Andy said, "Now give Mr. Doodle a large piece of chocolate cake because he must be hungry!" Marggy's mama did as Raggedy Andy said, so when Mr. Doodle reached for the large piece of chocolate cake, he had to drop Raggedy

Andy's magic wooden sword, because Mr. Doodle had both hands full of cake and cookies.

"Whee!" Raggedy Andy cried as he picked up the magic wooden sword. "Now I have the wooden sword and Mr. Doodle cannot follow us. As soon as we finish eating our lunch, we will start again!"

This made Mr. Doodle feel so badly to think how easily Raggedy Andy had fooled him, he cried, and Raggedy Ann had to wipe the tears to keep them from spoiling Mr. Doodle's cake and cookies. Then Raggedy Ann wiped the crumbs from everyone's mouths and said, "It is time we hurried along."

So Raggedy Andy helped Marggy and her mama and Raggedy Ann upon the back of the paper dragon and then climbed up himself, "All right, Mister Paper Dragon!" Raggedy Andy called. "You can wiggle along through the woods as fast as you wish." Then the paper dragon started moving; slow at first, then faster and faster until he was going just as fast as it is possible for paper dragons to wiggle.

After they had ridden upon the Dragon's back for almost an hour, they came to a little house, and out across the road at the side of the house was a gate.

The Dragon came to a stop with his nose touching the gate, just as a man came out of the little house and said, "This is a toll gate, so you will have to pay one penny for each passenger and two pennies for the Dragon, if you wish to travel down the road."

"Dear me!" Raggedy Ann said to the man. "We haven't any pennies!"

"Then you must turn around and go back," the man said.

"But if we do not go further down the road, we shall never find Marggy's Daddy," Raggedy Ann said.

"That would be too bad," the man replied as he wiped the tears from his eyes. "But I must have a penny from each passenger and two for the Dragon before I can let you pass."

"I know what to do!" the Dragon cried. "I'll wiggle back the road and get a good start, then I'll jump right over the gate."

JOHNNY GRUELLE

"Oh no!" Raggedy Ann said. "That would be cheating if you did that! And every one knows it isn't fair to cheat. We must find the pennies somewhere."

"Hasn't that man back there any pennies?" the toll gate keeper asked as he pointed back towards the Dragon's tail. And when they looked back there sitting upon the dragon's tail they saw Mr. Doodle.

When he found that he was discovered riding upon the Dragon's tail, Mr. Doodle came up to the Dragon's head and asked, "How much is it, Mr. Tollgate Keeper?"

"One penny for each passenger and two pennies for the Dragon," the Tollgate Keeper replied.

Mr. Doodle looked through all his pockets but could only find two pennies, a shoe button and a wire nail, "Dear me!" Mr. Doodle said. "I only have two pennies and that is only enough to take the Dragon through the tollgate."

"What shall we do?" Marggy's mama asked. "We can never find Marggy's daddy unless we go farther down the road!"

The tollgate keeper took off his hat and scratched his head. Finally he said, "I'll tell you how we can let you go through the tollgate. You know we charge only for people who ride, so if you hop down from the Dragon's back, I will charge two pennies for the Dragon and the rest of you can walk through the tollgate."

"We are very glad that you happened to think of that before we turned back," Raggedy Andy laughed as he jumped from the Dragon's back and helped Marggy and her mama and Raggedy Ann down.

Marggy's mama gave the toll gate keeper six cookies and a piece of chocolate cake and this pleased the Tollgate Keeper so much he asked every one, except the Dragon, who was too large, into his house and gave them each a glass of soda water, for you see, the Tollgate Keeper owned a little store too, so that anyone passing could have candy and peanuts and popcorn and lollypops and ice cream sodas.

Then Mr. Doodle, who was very fond of ice cream sodas asked the Tollgate Keeper if he would trade a lot of soda water for the shoe button and wire nail.

The Tollgate Keeper said that he had always longed for a shoe button and a wire nail, so he gave every one a soda and a bag of peanuts and took the shoe button and wire nail.

"I really believe Mr. Doodle has forgotten he wanted to take the Dragon home for a chicken coop," Raggedy Ann whispered to Raggedy Andy.

"I believe so, too!" Raggedy Andy whispered in return to Raggedy Ann. "For if he had not paid the Tollgate Keeper the two pennies to get the Dragon through the tollgate, he could have taken the Dragon away from us again."

But Raggedy Andy did not remind Mr. Doodle of this. Mr. Doodle laughed and talked with everyone and said he was sorry he did not have another shoe button and a wire nail he could trade for more sodas and peanuts.

"Well," Mr. Doodle said, when he had finished drinking the last of his soda. "I guess we had better be going on, or it will be late before we find Marggy's Daddy!"

After shaking hands with the kind Tollgate Keeper the Dragon carried them through the woods until they came to a great marble castle.

CHAPTER TEN

IN FRONT of the great marble castle stood a Knight all dressed in shiny armor and he had a great big shiny sword. When the Dragon stopped in front of the Knight, the Knight whirled his sword close to the Dragon's nose.

"Please be careful, Mr. Knight," Raggedy Ann said. "You might cut off the Dragon's nose."

"Ha!" the Knight laughed as he whirled his sword again. "Little would I care if I did! We have a prisoner shut up in the castle and I must guard the door so that no one can get in and rescue him."

"I'll bet a nickel the prisoner is Marggy's Daddy," Mr. Doodle said.

"It is!" the Knight cried. "And if you know what is good for you, you will turn around and run as fast as you can!"

"Please do be careful," Raggedy Ann again said. "You almost whacked the paper Dragon that time! It wouldn't be nice for you to cut off his nose even if it is only paper!"

"Then if you will hop down from the Dragon's back, I will cut off your nose," the Knight said to Raggedy Ann.

"Indeed you won't," Raggedy Ann laughed. "For my nose is merely painted upon my face and it can't be cut off."

"Then I will cut off that man's nose," the Knight said as he pointed his sword at Mr. Doodle.

"But I do not care to have my nose cut off!"

"Then I shall cut off your nose anyhow!" The Knight shouted. "So if you do not wish your nose cut off you had better run as fast as you know how!"

"I will not run a step!" Mr. Doodle cried. "And if you try to cut off my nose, I shall try to cut off your nose too, only you will have to lend me your sword."

"Ha, ha, ha!" the Knight laughed. "I would be foolish to do that! You have a sword," pointing to Raggedy Andy's wooden sword. "Take that and we will have a grand fight to see which one cuts off the other's nose."

Raggedy Andy loaned Mr. Doodle his magic wooden sword and Mr. Doodle walked towards the Knight.

"Wait a minute," the Knight said. "Someone will have to fasten my helmet down so Mr. Doodle cannot cut off my nose!"

"That is only fair," Mr. Doodle replied. "For I know you do not wish your nose cut off any more than I wish mine cut off, so I will fasten your helmet."

"There!" Mr. Doodle said when he finished fastening the Knight's helmet. "Now I cannot even see your eyes."

"But I cannot see out of the helmet either!" the Knight howled. "And how can I fight you when I can't see?"

"Well!" Mr. Doodle replied. "You said you wanted the helmet fastened down tight so now you will have to make the best of it!" And as Mr. Doodle winked at Raggedy Andy, he hit the Knight's helmet so hard with the wooden sword it sounded like someone had kicked a tin dish pan.

"Oh! My nose! Oh, my nose!" the Knight howled and every time he howled, Mr. Doodle hit the Knight's helmet harder than ever with the wooden sword until the Knight threw down his shiny sword and cried, "Let's quit fighting! I have changed my mind, I shall not cut off your nose!"

"Thank you!" Mr. Doodle said as he winked at Raggedy Ann and unfastened the Knight's helmet.

"My goodness! I did not know anyone could fight so good with just a wooden sword!" the Knight said. "You won the fight very quickly!"

"Maybe if you had not fastened your helmet down over your eyes, you could have won the fight," Mr. Doodle said. "Shall we try it again without the helmet?"

"No, thank you," the Knight replied. "I feel certain that if I do not have the helmet fastened down tight over my face you will be sure to cut off my nose. You see, I try to frighten people away from the castle by pretending that I am a great fighter, but really, I am always very timid, for I have a real tender heart."

"And you did not intend cutting off Mr. Doodle's nose?" Raggedy Ann asked.

"Dear me, no!" the Knight laughed. "You see, I shut my eyes anyway when I fight, so I could not have cut off Mr. Doodle's nose for I could not have seen it!"

"I am glad you are so kind hearted," Raggedy Ann said. "Really, that is the best way to be anyhow."

"That is just what my mama has always told me," the Knight said. "And now that Mr. Doodle has won the fight there is nothing to keep you from going into the castle unless it is the two-headed dog just inside the door. He may jump out and chase you away when you open the door."

"We will go and knock upon the door," Mr. Doodle said. "Then if the two-headed dog barks, we will know enough not to open the door."

"Oh, he barks something terrible," the Knight said. "It makes cold chills run up my neck when I hear him bark."

"You don't 'spect the two-headed dog has eaten up my daddy, do you?" Marggy asked.

"Oh, my no!" the Knight replied. "I saw your daddy looking out of a window awhile ago! No! The two-headed dog hasn't eaten him up."

Mr. Doodle walked up to the door and the Dragon wiggled along with the others.

"Why! There is the little ball of red darning cotton!" Raggedy Ann cried as she pointed to the door step. "Please

JOHNNY GRUELLE

hand it to me, Mr. Doodle; it got away ahead of us when you delayed us so many times!"

"I am very sorry!" Mr. Doodle said as he handed the ball of red darning cotton to Raggedy Ann.

"Knock on the door, it wouldn't be polite to walk in without knocking," Raggedy Andy suggested. "What we want to do is to get in the castle and rescue Marggy's Daddy who has been inside as a prisoner for so long, but if the dog barks then we are as bad off as we are now."

"I know what to do," Mr. Doodle suggested. "Let's hammer upon the castle door with the wooden sword and the two-headed dog will stay at the door in hopes that we will open it and let him out, but we will fool him! While someone hammers on the door and keeps the two-headed dog there I will run around in back and climb up the water pipe to one of the windows, then I'll tip-toe down and throw a blanket, or something, over the dog's two heads and unlock the door for you to come in!"

"That is a good idea," Raggedy Ann said. "Let's go and hammer on the door with the wooden sword."

The Dragon carried them all up to the door of the castle upon his back and Raggedy Andy hammered upon the castle door with his magic wooden sword. WHACK! WHACK! WHACK!

Then they heard the loudest barks they had ever heard from a dog.

"My goodness!" Raggedy Ann cried. "He must be very, very large to bark so loud! I am afraid if you climb up the pipes and tip-toe down to throw something over the dog's two heads, you will not find a blanket large enough!"

"I have a better idea," the Dragon said. "Mr. Doodle might fall and hurt himself. I will open my mouth as wide as I can, then when you open the door, the great two headed dog will jump right out into my mouth, then I'll close my mouth and we will have him a prisoner!"

"Hm!" mused Raggedy Andy. "Suppose the two-headed

dog starts scratching and biting after he jumps into your mouth?"

"I won't mind that!" the Dragon replied. "You can get inside the door long before he tears the paper off my sides and gets out, and I will be glad to do this for Marggy's sake."

So the Dragon opened his mouth so wide it covered the whole door and Raggedy Andy poked the magic wooden sword between the Dragon's paper teeth and pushed the castle door open. There came five very, very, loud barks as the two-headed dog jumped out of the door into the Dragon's mouth. Then the Dragon's mouth closed shut with a snap and the two-headed dog was a prisoner.

MY! How the two-headed dog scratched around inside the Dragon. He made a lot of noise, because the Dragon was made of slats and covered with heavy paper.

"Now we must jump off the Dragon's back and hunt through the castle until we find Marggy's Daddy. And we must hurry before the great two-headed dog chews the paper out of the Dragon's side and chases us!" Raggedy Ann cried.

"After we find Marggy's Daddy, then the Dragon can open his mouth and let the two-headed dog out, for after we find Marggy's Daddy, then, of course, there will be no reason for the dog guarding the door, and he will probably run around the castle and hunt for a bone to eat!" Mr. Doodle said.

"Maybe it would be a good plan giving the dog a bone before we go into the castle," Raggedy Ann suggested. "For if the dog has something to eat, then he won't tear the paper off of the Dragon's wooden slats." Everyone thought this was a good idea. Raggedy Ann usually thought of the best way of doing everything. But, of course, when they looked through all their pockets, not even Mr. Doodle had a bone.

"We will have to give the two-headed dog a large piece of chocolate cake," Marggy's Mama said. "All I have in my basket is cake and cookies and I do not believe that will be enough for such a large two-headed dog."

"Then we must give him two pieces of chocolate cake," said Raggedy Ann. "One for each head."

So Marggy's Mama cut off two large pieces of chocolate cake and told the Dragon to open his mouth. "Just as soon as the great two-headed dog sees that he can get out, then he will quit his loud barking and I will throw him the cake," she said.

So the Dragon opened his mouth and Marggy's Mama tossed the two pieces of cake where the two-headed dog could see them.

"Look out!" the Dragon cried, "He's coming out!" and out from the Dragon's mouth came the two-headed dog.

When Raggedy Ann saw the two-headed dog, she jumped from the Dragon's back and caught the dog in her arms, for the two-headed dog which guarded the castle door with such a loud bark was only six inches high, and the cutest little creature the Raggedys had ever seen.

Raggedy Ann held the two-headed dog in her arms while Raggedy Andy and Marggy and her Mama and Mr. Doodle fed him small pieces of cookies and chocolate cake. My! How Raggedy Ann laughed!

After the two-headed dog had eaten all the cake he wanted, Raggedy Ann wiped the crumbs from his two mouths with her apron and said, "Now that we have discovered that the two-headed dog is only a little teeny, weeny dog we can take him with us through the castle and hunt for Marggy's Daddy!"

"I will be glad to go with you," the two-headed dog said out of both of his mouths at the same time. "For I know just where Marggy's Daddy is!"

"It is funny that the people who own this castle had such a tiny, little two-headed dog to guard the door," Raggedy Andy said.

"But, you see," the little two-headed dog explained. "I have just about the largest bark in the world, and when I stand at the door and bark, whoever is outside thinks, 'Goodness gracious! That must be a very large dog!' And of course that frightens them away!"

"Yes," agreed Raggedy Ann. "We thought you must be almost as large as a horse when we heard you bark. Are you a magic dog?"

JOHNNY GRUELLE.

"Oh, yes," the little two-headed dog replied. "Everything in the castle is magic. That is why Marggy's Daddy stays at the castle instead of going home."

"I do not understand!" Marggy's Mama said. "Why does he have to stay at the magic castle, little two-headed dog?"

"Because," the little dog replied. "When Marggy's Daddy is in the castle, he can remember you and Marggy and everyone he knew before, but just as soon as he starts to go out of the castle door, he loses his memory and while he is outside the castle he forgets about everyone he knew. So you see he stays in the castle so that he can always remember you."

"Then," Raggedy Ann wondered. "Perhaps we had better not go inside the magic castle, or we may lose our memory."

"No," the little dog said. "The magic only works on people who enter the castle on Monday."

"If that is the case, let us all go inside, for today is Wednesday," Mr. Doodle cried. "And when we are once inside, perhaps we can find Marggy's Daddy's memory and give it back to him after we get him outside of the magic castle."

Raggedy Ann, Raggedy Andy, Mr. Doodle, Marggy and her Mama all walked down the long hall and through an open door, and there, sitting in a comfortable chair was Marggy's Daddy. Marggy and her Mama ran to him and threw their arms about him, but he looked so surprised, everyone knew that Marggy's Daddy did not know Marggy and her Mama.

"Don't you recognize Marggy and her Mama?" Raggedy Ann asked.

"No! I cannot remember ever seeing them before!" Marggy's Daddy replied.

CHAPTER ELEVEN

"I'LL just bet a nickel that he has lost his memory around the castle somewhere," Raggedy Andy said.

"But I had my memory when I came in a few minutes ago!" Marggy's Daddy said.

"Well! You haven't it now!" Raggedy Ann replied. "So tell us just where you have been about the castle and we will try and find your memory for you."

So Marggy's Daddy led the way to the Wonder Room, but no one could find his memory. Then they searched through the dining room, but it was not there!

"I had it when I came in the back door," Marggy's Daddy said.

Raggedy Ann ran to the easy chair where they had first seen Marggy's Daddy and there, sticking between the pages of a book to mark the place where he had been reading, was Marggy's Daddy's memory. Then everyone was very happy and Marggy's Daddy took them all on his lap and hugged them, even Mr. Doodle.

"Tell us how you happened to be a prisoner in the magic castle, Daddy," Marggy said as she gave him a hug.

"One day," Marggy's Daddy began, "I kissed Marggy and her Mama good-bye and started down to the store and when I came to a great tree which had fallen across the road, I heard someone talking inside."

"Who was it, Daddy?" Marggy wished to know.

"It was a little gnome, sitting there smoking his pipe and talking to himself," Marggy's Daddy went on. "And I heard him talking about a wonderful Magic Castle, with a great room in it called the Wonder Room. And I heard him tell just how to find the Magic Castle. So instead of going to the grocery I walked through the woods until I came to this castle. The two-headed dog barked so loud at the front door, I went around to the back door and as it was open, I walked right inside. But whenever I went outside of the castle, I lost my memory. So I couldn't think to return to Marggy and her Mama. But when I came back into the Magic Castle, then I could remember them. So, rather than leave the castle and forget them, I had to stay here all the time, so that I could think of them."

"Now that we have found you, Daddy," Marggy's Mama said, "Let's return home!"

"That is just what I was thinking of," Marggy's Daddy replied. "And just as soon as I pack a few magic things in a suit case, we will start. I have found so many wonderful magic things in the Wonder Room, I hardly know which to take home."

Of course, everyone wished to know what the wonderful things were, so Marggy's Daddy told them. "There is a magic clock," he said, "which strikes every five minutes. And as soon as it quits striking, it either tells a fairy story, or it sings a beautiful song. Then this book which I was reading when you came in is a wonderful book, too, for, while you read the story, you can see moving pictures of everything you read about. Then when you grow tired of reading yourself, it will read itself, right out loud!"

"That will be a nice book for Marggy to have," Marggy's Mama said.

"Yes, we must take it for Marggy," Marggy's Daddy agreed.

"Then, the magic soda water fountain in the Wonder

Room. We need it in our front room so that we can give everyone who comes in a nice ice cream soda. Then, there is a whole case of wonderful wishing rings. We each need one. And there is a wonderful invisible cloak, which makes anyone invisible. Then there are magical roller skates, which when fastened to your shoes, will carry you around as fast, or as slow as you wish to go."

Then Marggy's Daddy got a very large suitcase, for it had to be very large to get all the magical things inside. Everyone helped Marggy's Daddy pack the magical things in the suitcase.

"Now, I guess we are all ready to start," Marggy's Daddy laughed as he took the suitcase upon his shoulder.

"What have you in the suitcase?" the Dragon asked as he saw Marggy's Daddy with the suitcase on his shoulder.

"Some wonderful things I picked up inside," Marggy's Daddy replied. Then a queer look came over his face and he put the suitcase upon the ground and opened it.

"I thought so!" he cried. "I felt it suddenly grow light, and it had been so heavy before; all the wonderful things have disappeared!"

"The magic soda water fountain, too?" Marggy asked.

"Yes! It has disappeared, too! Now we can't take them home and enjoy them!"

"Well!" Raggedy Andy mused. "It seems to me that the wonderful Magic Castle has been made so that whoever enters the Magic Castle can enjoy the wonderful magical things in the Wonder Room, but if everyone who goes into the Magic Castle carries away some of the wonderful things, in a very short time, there would be nothing left. And so, the magical things always come back to the Wonder Room."

"That is so!" agreed Marggy's Daddy. "And it was not right for us to take them."

"Indeed, it wasn't," Raggedy Andy said. "You must keep the wonderful magic castle for your home."

"Whee! Whee!" Marggy's Daddy cried, "Raggedy Andy

has thought of the nicest way! We will all live in the magic Castle where we can all enjoy the magic things in the Wonder Room; the magic soda water fountain, the wishing rings, the talking books, the magic clock and all the other wonderful things, and Raggedy Ann and Raggedy Andy and Mr. Doodle and the Dragon can live here with us!"

They all caught hold of hands and danced around in a circle. All except Mr. Doodle, and as everyone looked at Mr. Doodle, they saw great big salty tears running down his nose and falling to the ground. "Why, Mr. Doodle!" Raggedy Ann cried, "Whatever is the trouble?"

It was a long time before Mr. Doodle could reply and it would have been much longer than that if Marggy's Mama hadn't given him a piece of chocolate cake out of her basket. After Mr. Doodle had eaten the chocolate cake, Raggedy Ann said, "Tell us why you weep, Mr. Doodle."

"Because," Mr. Doodle replied. "Because, you will remember, I wanted to take the paper Dragon home and use him for a chicken coop. He is hollow all the way to the tip of his tail, and he would make a lovely chicken coop. But now, I know the paper Dragon is such a kind creature, I do not wish to take him away from you and take him home, besides, if I did that, there would be no one to guard the outside doors of the Magic Castle."

"But," Marggy's Mama said, "You are going to stay

right here in the wonderful Magic Castle with us, and if you do that, there is no need of you having a chicken coop. For, every time you wish fried chicken, all you will have to do will be to wish for it and you will have it. Isn't that so, Daddy?"

"Indeed, it is true," Marggy's Daddy replied. "So dry your tears, Mr. Doodle and live with us in the Magic Castle and we will have a lot of fun."

"Then I must run home and get Mrs. Doodle," Mr. Doodle said as he wiped the last tear from his eye.

"Do not pack anything in your suitcases," Marggy's Daddy advised. "For if you, or Mrs. Doodle, want new clothes any time, all you have to do is wish for them."

"I shall not bring a thing except Mrs. Doodle," Mr. Doodle laughed. "Now just see how fast I can run home and return with Mrs. Doodle."

"I'll bet a nickel it won't take him very long," Raggedy

Andy laughed, as they watched Mr. Doodle run away through the woods toward his home.

In a very short time Mr. Doodle came running back with Mrs. Doodle, for he had hardly got started running through the woods when he met Mrs. Doodle coming after him.

"I just thought Mr. Doodle never would come home," Mrs. Doodle laughed when she was introduced to everyone. "Is it true that you wish Mr. Doodle and me to live in this beautiful castle with you, even after Mr. Doodle and I treated you so mean?"

"Yes, indeed, Mrs. Doodle!" Marggy's Mama said. "You see, Mr. Doodle has changed quite a lot since you saw him last, and if it had not been for his kindness to us, we would never have found our nice Daddy."

"Then I am so happy!" Mrs. Doodle said as she wept on Raggedy Ann's shoulder. "Papa Doodle has always been a very lazy Papa and that was one reason why he always wanted to capture Marggy. He really wanted her to do the work!"

"And I know just how naughty I was, Mama Doodle," Mr. Doodle said. "And I have promised myself that I shall chop every piece of wood we need in the nice, wonderful Magical Castle to cook with."

"Aha!" Marggy's Daddy laughed as he gave Mr. Doodle a friendly thump upon the back. "We will need no wood around here to cook with, my friend, for if we wish fried chicken or doughnuts or anything, we do not have to build a fire and cook. No, sir!"

So Marggy's Daddy led the way into the dining room of the castle and everyone wished for just whatever they liked best for supper. And you may be certain that everyone got exactly what they wished for, too, because that was the way things worked in the wonderful castle. After supper, everyone went into the Wonder Room and listened to the Magic Book as it read fairy tales out loud, and while they listened to the fairy tales they all had a great many ice cream sodas.

"It is really time we were all getting to bed," Marggy's Daddy said. "The earlier we go to bed, the earlier we can get up in the morning, and think how much fun we shall have then."

Marggy's Daddy knew every room in the great castle, so he showed everyone just where to sleep, then when he had wound the clock and covered up the canary bird and saw the little two-headed dog had gone to his box, Marggy's Daddy went to bed, too.

"Wasn't it just like a Fairy Tale?" Raggedy Ann asked Raggedy Andy as they put on their nighties and hopped into bed.

"Indeed, it was, Raggedy Ann," Raggedy Andy laughed. "And I 'spect, just like all nice Fairy Tales, everyone will live happily together here in the wonderful Magic Castle forever."

And the two Raggedys, their shiny shoe button eyes looking happily at the ceiling, felt in their little cotton stuffed bodies that indeed, this would prove true, for unhappiness can never creep in when hearts are filled with the sunshine of unselfish love.

Raggedy Ann and Raggedy Andy have a good time in their books and so does everybody who reads them. Their adventures in "Raggedy Ann's Wishing Pebble" and "Raggedy Ann and the Camel With the Wrinkled Knees" are as funny and interesting as "Raggedy Ann and the Paper Dragon." You will want to own the Raggedy Ann and Raggedy Andy books and a Raggedy Ann and Raggedy Andy Bookshelf to put them on.